I WAS NEVER AFRAID

SCOTT BAKER SWEENEY

authorHOUSE®

AuthorHouse™
1663 Liberty Drive
Bloomington, IN 47403
www.authorhouse.com
Phone: 1 (800) 839-8640

Published by AuthorHouse 01/05/2017

ISBN: 978-1-5246-4829-9 (sc)
ISBN: 978-1-5246-4830-5 (hc)
ISBN: 978-1-5246-4828-2 (e)

Library of Congress Control Number: 2016918221

Print information available on the last page.

CHAPTER 1

A blood curdling scream intermixed with hysterical demonic laugher echoed through the long narrow corridors of the asylum. Somehow the faint sound of a chirping wheel from a medicine cart was still audible. It found its way to a young girl's ear, as she lay curled up on a mattress in a dreary small room, half the length of the building away. To most, the disturbing vocal medley would be all they could hear or tolerate, but this child seemed to be accustomed to these disturbing sounds, as if they were a regular part of her life for a long time. One would only conclude that she subconsciously had learned to filter the unpleasant noise and tether on to any sound that wasn't repugnant.

The faulty wheel of the cart, the source of the chirping, was a familiar as well as an anticipated noise for the child. Her eyes opened wide and she sat up in bed. She knew it announced the arrival of a tall nun. Medications were distributed each and every morning before breakfast to the patients to whom they were prescribed. The sister would dispense the tablets through a slot in the door and remain peering through the small security window, long enough to view the consumption, before moving on to the next door.

The cart finally rolled in front of the little girl's door, but instead of pale blue pills in the paper receptacle, it had a Tootsie Roll candy. The contents slid through the slot in the door and a tiny hand reached out to collect the chocolate prize.

Her eyes sparkled with delight and a smile took form on her face as she examined the candy. The observation window in the door was too high for her to see out without standing on a chair, but the six inch slot was not, so she drew her face close to catch a peek at her kind friend. Oddly she saw nothing but the metal cart. She tilted her head to peer in the other direction but still, no nun.

Surmising that the nun surely could hear her, even though she was out of sight, the child raised her head slightly so that her mouth was now in front of the slot. "Thank you," she spoke No reply. Well for good measure, she'd try again, "Thank you, Sister," at a louder pitch.

Still, no response. With a smile on her face, staring at the candy in her hand she kept her head within inches of the opening listening for the nun's return. There was the chirp again! Once again, the girl leaned over to convey her appreciation when a hand shot through the opening, grabbing her by the throat, lifting her to her toes and pulling her to the door. Her head crashed against the door and her arms began to flail sending the roll of chocolate flying.

CHAPTER 2

Carolina sat straight up in bed, her sheets already kicked off by the thrashing of her legs, her face glistened and her sweat soaked nightshirt clung to her frame. She took a deep breath to gather her wits and settle her pounding heart and then turned to glance at her clock on the nightstand. Exhaling a breath, she ran her hands through her hair then crawled out of bed. It was a little earlier than she normally woke, but there was no way she could sleep after this dream. She cautiously walked to the window and opened the blinds introducing the early dawn light to her dark room. The natural light exposed the clutter of boxes and articles of clothing that littered the floor, reminding her of the unfinished task of unpacking.

Carolina was a new resident to this apartment. Her new casa was merely a cubby hole of just three rooms, a bedroom, a small kitchen and a bath, but it was convenient and cheap. It was located directly above a quaint bicycle repair shop and a short bus or bike ride to her new job at the *Denver Post*. She stared out the window, but was oblivious to the view. She might as well have been staring at a bare wall. She was intensely preoccupied with analyzing her dream, the same reoccurring dream that started soon after she moved to this new place. It was terribly chilling and surreal, she thought, every night a different scene from the same saga and always involving the same little girl. But why?" Carolina struggled for answers.

Carolina broke from her deep self psychoanalysis by the buzz of her alarm clock. She would have to wait until later to search for answers on her subconscious brain behavior, at this moment she had to get ready for work. "Work, indeed! Three months into my new career, overflowing with enthusiasm and armed with a fresh degree in journalism from the University of Notre Dame and all I have to show for it is a story on soccer moms, new grade school lunch programs and a missing cat." Carolina smiled, climbing into the shower, thinking of her email she sent to her sister the day before. When she climbed out of the shower, she mumbled her sister's reply. "Patience and perseverance, Carolina!"

With lip-gloss in one hand and her cell phone in the other, Carolina shot out her door and down the outside staircase. As part of her morning routine she floated past the bicycle store window to give a smile and flirtatious finger wave to her not so inconspicuous bicycle mechanic fan club waiting for her procession. As she strutted past them, they waved back in unison and gawked at her all the way to the corner bus stop.

For as long as Carolina Paige could remember she wanted to be a journalist. No one in her family was a journalist, none of her friends were journalists, she never even met a journalist until she interned as a Senor for her home town newspaper. Never the less, at an early age, she had a strong desire to find out the truth and then write about it.

Carolina's parents conceived her while on a camping trip to the Outer Banks, nine months later they had no choice but to name her Carolina.

By the age of eight she grew into a real nuisance for her brothers and sister. Carolina followed them around with pencil and paper, jotting down everything they said or did and leave copies of her report on her parents bed, as if it were her editor's desk. Two years later and with the chagrin of her parents Carolina cracked the Santa Claus mystery wide open. Christmas mornings were never the same from that point on. Of course her early prowess followed her through academia; she was the editor of the school paper at high school and at Notre Dame.

Getting accepted to Notre Dame and finishing Cum Laude was no easy accomplishment but it was a paramount step toward achieving her goal of landing a job at a major paper or television news network. Carolina's ambitious objective was ultimately becoming syndicated as her own entity, but she knew that would only come with years of seasoned experience. She had several job offers from papers in large metropolitan cities such as Chicago, Pittsburgh and her hometown of Indianapolis, but she chose the *Denver Post* after her research revealed that a couple of senor journalists were near retirement. Carolina felt she could advance up the ranks quicker there.

"Paige, see me in my office in five!" This poignant statement from Carolina's boss penetrated the elevator compartment before the door had a chance to completely open. Being greeted by the managing editor, Martin (Marty) Whitten first thing in the morning provided more stimulus than four cups of coffee. His spontaneous command caught her by surprise as they passed almost brushing shoulders at the opening of the stainless steel doors of the elevator.

"Yes Sir!" She replied, turning and watching him push the button to his floor. Carolina remained poised waiting for further directions that never came before the door shut.

"This is odd," she thought as she hurried to her cubicle to drop off her coat and grab her laptop. "I must be in trouble for something that I've written and now he wants me to write my first retraction." Endless impulsive scenarios were now stinging her brain.

Carolina's reactionary response as she headed to the managerial floors was to start preparing her retort to anything that would be thrown at her.

Even though it was a smoke-free building the stench of stale cigarettes was definite and apparent on the management floor. The abhorrent scent was transported from the outside by the clothes of the smokers. The bouquet that this floor gave off was a much different aroma than the lower floors occupied daily by younger and more health conscience workers. Carolina anticipated the stale musty air and took in a deep breath before entering the area. She then made a bee line directly for Whitten's office.

"Sit down Ms. Paige and close the door."

Carolina took her place in the large black leather chair facing her boss across the desk. She placed her laptop securely on her legs but never releasing her grip.

"Here's what I've got," Growled Whitten. His gruff bark caused Carolina to grip her laptop tighter. "Well, let me start by saying I've had my eye on you ever since your first story landed on my desk. I know that statement sounds cliché and probably not very PC, 'the eye on you' part, but what the Hell? I don't remember the content of the article other than it was very well written. It actually grabbed by attention and I thought your word flow was exceptional." It was apparent that Whitten was uneasy with his praise of Carolina, so he stood and walked to the window. "This old editor has never had a PC filter and I'm not about to get one now. You will find out that I'm very direct and all I want is for you to be very direct right back at me. Bullshitting is such a time waster and time is valuable. You can always give back bullshit, but you can never give back time. Remember that when you write too! Be descriptive, concise and succinct, in other words Paige, get to the point quick. This free advice is something that most professors overlook. The new college shits they send me can type several pages of well written bland and boring. There's no excitement in their words, no passion in their prose. They can't even put together an interesting thought let alone write a compelling article. They're proficient at incoherent babbling! Well look at me now, I'm the one babbling." Whitten turned from the window, smiled and sat down.

"It's time Paige that you got your first shot at a major story. Are you ready to write me something with excitement and passion?" Whitten asked.

"Yes Sir and thank you Sir." Carolina released some of her grip on her laptop. Whitten leaned forward in his chair as if to make certain she understood his next statement.

"Ms. Paige, the problem I have with my younger journalists pales in comparison to the problems I've been having lately with some of my veteran journalists. They can't keep their damn mouths shut. They end up leaking what they're working on to the TV news before the print comes across my desk. I can't tell you how long it's been since we had an exclusive. Half the time I can't even get credit for the story.

"I understand, Sir." Carolina responded.

Whitten eased back in his chair and nodded his head. "Last week while sifting through my unread emails and my weekly pile of passionately, authored letters from alien abductees, Elvis's neighbor and the guy who has proof that the Governor is a zombie, I came across an envelope that caught my eye. It was postmarked from Bogotá Colombia, so I opened and discovered the note inside was even more interesting.

"So Paige, I want you to investigate Denver's Homeless Coalition." I want you to follow the money trails, contributions going in and expenditures going out. Where, who and why, you get it? I'm not ready to divulge the contents of the letter quite yet, or the significance of where it came from. I want to conduct my own investigations first and also I don't want to bias anything you find on your own. The city accounting records are open and should be public and accessible. Don't draw too much attention to yourself when you're nosing around. Denver's Homeless Coalition is very popular with the politicians and most of the Mile High City citizens are very proud of its accomplishments. Popular and proud are two adjectives that tend to make people very sensitive and protective. Our angle should be that we merely want to promote the cause and help increase contributions. Studying trends in contributions will help us with that. Do some digging and get back to me. Now go!"

Excited by his closing command Carolina jumped up vaulting her laptop from her cradled hands. Luckily, she was able to secure it with her figure tips at the last moment saving it from certain annihilation against the hard floor.

"Thanks for your confidence in me sir, I will get right to work." Carolina concealed her excitement as best she could exiting Whitten's office, but once the elevator door closed she let go a jubilant cry of "YES!"

Carolina wasted no time. She briefly visited her cubicle to gather her credentials and then she was on her way to the Denver City and County Building.

CHAPTER 3

Her quick cab ride gave her just enough time to Google 'Denver's Homeless Coalition' to familiarize herself with the basics. Metro Denver Homeless Coalition or MDHC, is an independently funded, non-profit organization whose noble mission is to end homelessness in Denver and the surrounding counties. "Independently funded yes, but very politically linked," Carolina thought to herself as she continued to read. In October 2003, Mayor Arthur Higgins appointed members to the Denver Commission.

As the cab pulled to the curb, Carolina closed her computer and handed the driver her fare. Before she exited the vehicle she glanced at the long steps leading up to the massive limestone City and County building. She thought to herself, "Today I'm not a reporter, I'm an explorer."

"May I help you?" A seasoned silver-haired man greeted Carolina as she approached the information desk in the center the rotunda.

"It's hard to sneak up on anyone wearing hard soled-shoes on this marble floor," Carolina responded to her loud clopping walk.

"Yes, it's like working inside an echo chamber. The man responded with a grin. "How can I help you Hun?"

"Can you direct me to the office of Denver's Homeless Coalition?"

Without hesitation the man unfolded his arms and pointed up. "Dear, they're right above us on the second floor." Carolina thanked him then walked toward the elevators. "When you get up there you tell Mrs. Elizabeth that Mr. James is surely missing her delicious apple cobbler." Carolina turned and acknowledged his comment with a smile.

Carolina walked to the second floor corridor of glass doors until she found the office.

"Good Morning, I'm Carolina Paige from the *Denver Post*." Carolina reached in her purse pulling out her crisp bright identification card and presented it to a lady behind the desk. The silver-haired lady was unimpressed with Carolina's first ever professional introduction. Instead she looked directly over her reading glasses; past Carolina's ID and glared with disgust directly into the young reporter's eyes. The awkward silence seemed eternal.

"I hear you make a mean apple cobbler." This was all that Carolina could think of to break the ice.

The lady reached up and removed her reading glasses and exposed a meager smile.

"I see that you've met that old coot downstairs. The lady shook her head. "I'll dread the day that I got him that job."

"You must know him well," Carolina queried.

"Know him, oh brother, she rolled her eyes. "I know him too well. I'm married to him." I'm Elizabeth Sanders, and I am the office manager for the Denver Homeless Coalition. So, Ms Paige from the *Denver Post*, what can I do for you?" Carolina's clever comeback of the apple cobbler was enough to break the ice with the irritable gatekeeper.

"I would like to do some research for an upcoming feature in the *Post* regarding the success of Denver's Homeless Coalition. How it started, how far it's grown, how many homeless people it's helped, etc, etc."

"Well, I don't do interviews, nor do any of my personnel. We're not the mayor's P.R. department; we just take the donations, document them, and disburse the proceeds to where ***they*** direct me."

"Who are they?" Carolina asked.

"The mayor's office, of course," Elizabeth snapped. Why don't you just talk to the mayor or any of his smiling do-gooders? They would be more than happy to fill your paper with quotes of self accolades. Besides, the Mayor has directed me to alert him personally if anyone from the press came nosing around."

"Alert him personally?" So why do you think that he's so protective of your commission? You're not exactly a clandestine agency," Carolina asked.

Elizabeth shrugged her shoulders, "I don't know. He mentioned privacy laws or something. I don't know, nor do I care! I don't ask questions that are none of my business. Once again, all this little office does is take in money and distribute money."

"I understand. I'm not wishing to cause any problems or get anyone in trouble. I was merely hoping to get some basic numbers, trends, demographics, that sort of stuff." Carolina replied.

Elizabeth looked at Carolina, took a deep breath then exhaled. "Okay Ms Paige, I don't know why I cause myself more work, but leave me your number and I'll see if I can get permission to give you some informational stats. As I explained, I need to get permission from the mayor himself, so it may take a few days. Mayor Higgins is in South America."

"South America?" Carolina sounded surprised

Elizabeth cocked her head looking puzzled. "Yes, Colombia. You should know this, your paper's always writing a piece regarding his annual fishing trips," She chucked. "I even remember one silly article, years back, comparing his expeditions to those of Ernest Hemingway. Yes, the mayor takes a few days a year and goes down to Bogotá, supposedly fishing with the mayor of Bogotá. But, I've never seen any pictures," she said under her breath.

"Hmm, I didn't know that. Well, I'm new to Denver and new to the *Post*."

"That would have been pertinent," Carolina thought to herself. She was now wondering why Whitten had not mentioned the mayors little excursions during their earlier discussion, especially if it was public knowledge.

"Well, thank you so much Mrs. Sanders. I'll be waiting for your call." Carolina handed her card, smiled and exited.

"Bogotá!" She whispered as she walked to the elevator. "Bogotá's in the middle of the country, not exactly a fishing port."

CHAPTER 4

The gait of Carolina's walk as she left the City and County Building was more deliberate than her entrance, flying past James with barely enough time to flash a smile. She hailed a cab and within minutes was back at the *Post* and inside her cubicle. Without hesitation she turned on her computer and logged into the internal server.

"Archives, here I come," Carolina muttered under her breath then focused on her task silently. As the hours went by her face drew closer to the computer screen. Carolina typed the words Mayor Higgins and Bogotá into the article search data base and immediately a plethora of articles dating back a decade appeared. Not really knowing what to look for she read them all, starting from the most recent. Finally, something caught her eye that provoked her to break her silence.

"You've got to be kidding me!" Carolina pushed herself away from her desk, jumped up and marched to the elevator to head to the managerial floor.

"Sir, may I have a minute?" Carolina pushed open Whitten's door with one hand while knocking with the other.

"What's up, Ms. Paige?" Whitten was hastily filling his briefcase and preparing to leave. He was now confronted by his irritated reporter standing in his doorway. His posture stiffened in defense and he stood upright. He looked at his watch and spouted a condescending remark, "Did you forget something from earlier today, or did you just forget to go home?"

"Oh I did forget something! I guess I forgot the part where you mentioned the mayor's fishing trips. You know, that little piece of knowledge could have been useful at the City and County Building," Carolina snapped.

Whitten walked around his desk, closed the door behind Carolina, and then walked directly in front of her, deliberately invading her personal space with his imposing girth.

"Ms Paige, I know you're a young spitfire and that's one of the reasons that I chose you. Regardless, let me explain how I expect our working relationship to work. You know, me the boss verses you the employee, relationship. First of all, the tone of your voice. We are not equals so I never want to hear that tone directed toward me again."

Carolina sighed, "I'm sorry sir. That came out a little more disrespectful than I intended. I was just a little frustrated being caught off guard at the Homeless Commission earlier."

"Caught off guard you say? Preparation is no one's responsibility but yours. Ms. Paige, your assignment was to collect data. You were the one who broke the number one rule of journalism; *always do your research first before rushing off to conduct interviews.* And that research doesn't include Google searching on your phone." Whitten glanced at Carolina clutching her phone then continued his lecture after sitting down at his desk.

"Oh hell, I guess that's why they invented microwaves, to warm up my supper. Sit!" He pointed to a chair and Carolina obeyed. "As you've just discovered, over the last ten years the paper has done several *feel good* articles of our beloved mayor and his deep sea fishing adventures."

"I wasn't always political editor. I started out like you, just one of several staff journalists. My job was to follow Mayor Higgins around and write weekly articles as to what he was doing. 'A more personal look that would interest the good citizens of Denver,' I believe were my boss orders. I took my assignment literally. Every morning when he walked into his office, there I'd be. I shadowed him everywhere. What a pain in the rear I was. They finally had to call my editor and tell them politely to have me back-off a little." Whitten chucked as he recalled this. "I did back off, only showing up once or twice a week, usually calling first to let his aides prepare for my arrival."

"I'm pretty sure now, that it was never their intent for me to find out about the South American fishing trips. Hell, as it turns out, very few people knew about them. One day before announcing my arrival at his office, I made a pit stop at the restroom. During my review of the daily topics from my stall, I heard two men enter the spacious tile commode. I assume they thought they were alone. I overheard a somewhat heated debate whether or not to have accompaniment to Bogotá. One of the voices I recognized as being that of the Mayor's. The last thing I heard him proclaim was, "I don't need an entourage to bait my hook." Then things got instantly quiet as I announced my presence with a flush followed immediately by the opening of the metal door. It was an awkward moment and very apparent that I was the last person on earth that either the mayor or his chief of staff wanted to be present at their little private party."

"Here was the scoop that I was waiting for. Mayor Higgins, big time fisherman!" Whitten paused again, mulling over his thoughts, then continued. "One time I even compared his sportsman-like exploits to that of Hemmingway. Ha!"

"On several occasions I asked to travel along with him, but my requests were always turned down. I could never find out exactly when he was leaving until after he was already gone. I even requested from the *Post* to allow me to try to follow him, but they always denied me, stating a lack in budgetary funds. By the way, I never bought the, 'budgetary funds' crap. We're the *Post* not some Podunk county paper. For God's sake he's the Mayor!" Whitten continued his rant.

"Not one picture of a fish was ever snapped!" Whiten shook his head. Carolina recalled that was almost verbatim the statement that Elizabeth made earlier. "Bogotá is on the wrong side of the Andes for deep sea fishing, and I never for once bought into the story. Eventually the *Post* stopped doing the pieces. I became editor and frankly forgot all about the Bogotá trips that is until now. Ms. Paige, I reread my articles, pretty benign and boring actually. I found nothing related to this recent letter, but you do your own digging. When it's time I'll show you the letter." Whitten opened up the door and followed Carolina to the elevator. She departed at her floor, but promised that she was merely turning off her computer before heading home.

Carolina reached over her desk to grab the mouse which inadvertently activated the black screen to the archives, as she left it before heading up to visit Whitten. Indeed it was the archives, but not the same date or article. The date was September 7, 1967 and the headline read '***Young Denver woman goes into the record books, completing 7300-mile Cross-Country bicycle Journey***'. Before Carolina could focus on the content it was gone from the screen and back to the mayor's South American fishing trip.

"I know, I know," She smiled at the subliminal reminder, and then quietly mumbled, "I need to get home to my little apartment above the bicycle shop."

CHAPTER 5

C arolina pecked on the window as she walked past the store to her staircase. Through the corner of her eye, she saw a chorus of acknowledging hand waves, and she smiled.

She made it a point everyday to announce her departure as well as her return to the crew at the shop. It wasn't just that she enjoyed flirting with the boys, which she did very much, she was also heeding the advice of her father. He advised her for safety reasons to make herself very visible, especially to people whom she could trust. Carolina did feel safe, at least during store hours. She took comfort knowing that below her apartment were a small group of males who were very interested in her routine and ready to demonstrate their chivalry to win her acceptance. Even though, she'd never conversed more than two sentences with any of them except Karl the store owner and her landlord, he and his starry-eyed mechanics were the closest thing to family she had this far away from home.

Kaleidospokes had been in business for more than sixty years. Proprietor Karl Kaleido was a second generation owner and a son of an immigrant. Karl was a wiry-framed blue-eyed, gentleman in his late 60's. His once jet black hair now a more seasoned salt and pepper. As a young man Karl aspired to be an Olympian. After waking at 4 a.m. to train, riding his Raleigh Sports Roadster twenty to thirty miles up brutal elevation grades in exhausting altitude, he'd report to work at his father's store and work late into the evening.

Carolina was fond of Karl. He always made time to chat, well in his case listen. Karl was very approachable, but a man of few words, so Carolina initiated most of the verbal banter. Each time she would visit she would uncover another fascinating piece of his bachelor past. It may have been her journalistic impulses or just her feminine instincts, but she found Karl a bit mysterious, and that intrigued her and left her compelled to learn more about him.

But, not tonight. Tonight she was more interested in a hot bath and then relaxing with a cup of hot cocoa. She grabbed her mail from the box on the side of the wall and up the stairs she went. After a brief moment of fumbling with her keys she was inside her casa. Kicking off her shoes and slipping out of her coat while shuffling through the envelopes of junk mail was a learned talent Carolina had mastered. Her fervent goal of shedding the work place stress by quickly getting comfortable was imperative. Within seconds the bath was running and within minutes she was submerged in the hot bubbly brew of tranquility. Carolina's eyes closed as she gently laid her head back against the tub, a smile formed on her face celebrating her fulfillment of complete Zen.

Her eyes rolled back into her head as she gasped for a breath, but the flow of oxygen was cut off by a hand clamping the windpipe in her throat. Her once convulsing legs were now limp. She did not hear the thrashing and screaming from the other side of the door as her unconscious body careened to the floor. Rattling keys preceded the large door opening with a fury. In rushed two nuns and a tall man in a white coat. The tiny child was whisked up and the group urgently exited the room, stepping over an overturned medicine cart and two other men in white coats restraining an individual on the floor. Her eyes were now wide open as she stared vacantly at the ceiling of the corridor. The sensation of floating, the distinct sound of multiple hard soled-shoes galloping on tiled floors and the light fixtures rapidly racing above her head were merely surreal to her half-conscience body. Her frame twitched repeatedly as she desperately tried to fill her lungs.

Panicked thoughts flooded Carolina's brain and she was now choking violently, unable to breathe. Her eyes flew open wide to a vision of blurry light. An eternity went by before Carolina realized she was staring up through water. She emerged from her watery grave choking and grasping for air. Her fear-induced response and rapid movement sent water flowing from the containment of the ceramic bathtub to the tile floor. She reached forward and pulled the plug draining the remainder of the warm soapy water, but remained sitting upright in the tub. Carolina's chest was heaving. She was still coughing and purging up bathwater. When she resumed her normal respiration and all her wits returned, she broke down. She cried for several minutes sitting naked and wet in the now empty and cold tub. She tried desperately to gather her emotions by using her journalistic skills to analyze the terrifying continuation of the dream she had the night earlier, but to no avail.

Carolina eventually composed herself long enough to call home and talk to her mother. Knowing that her mother was worried about her living alone in Denver, she was careful not to bring up her near drowning episode, but she did divulge her frequent dreams about the little girl. Of course her mother, like all mothers could sense the anxiety coming from her daughter's voice. They conversed for more than two hours and the comforting sound of her mother's voice did wonders to settle her down, but not enough to allow her to sleep that night.

"I might as well work," Carolina thought as she looked at the clock which now said 2:30 a.m. "I must be going insane," she thought as she opened her laptop.

"Bogotá Colombia," Carolina muttered as she began her search into Google. She began to read and absorb the data; Bogotá is the capital and largest city of Colombia and one of the biggest cities in Latin America. Its nearly eight million inhabitants can also boast they live in one of the highest, metropolitan areas in South America, at 8,612 feet above sea level. Bogotá is certainly a vast urban frenzy, that is, until it runs into the Andes Mountains. That's where the frenzy quietly ends. Bogotá practically has no mechanical industry, per say. The economy is mostly service driven, through various shops, stores, imports and exports. Modern Bogotá has gone to great lengths to change its crime rate and the surly image of its notorious drug commerce. A quote from one of the city fathers attempting to sum up the necessity of the change, "There was a fine line between a drug-war battlefield and a hip Bohemian city and Bogotá had crossed it." Taking credit for most of this image makeover was multi-term Mayor Luis Francisco Vargas. Carolina jotted his name on a Post It Note and stuck it on the corner of her keyboard.

"Oh, this is interesting," Carolina thought, as she caught a headline in her continued search. *'Bicycle Power in Bogotá'* encouraged by Bogotá's Mayor Vargas, every Sunday from seven a.m. to two p.m., more than seventy miles of streets in the city are open only to bicycles. "I'll have to recommend this as a vacation spot for Karl, the next time we talk," She thought and smiled.

When Whitten had teased her with the mysterious letter he received, Carolina immediately assumed it had something to do with illegal drug trade, so after learning the basic demographics she spent the rest of the night researching the web for South American drug cartels; who they were, how they interacted and their fundamental business model. Tomorrow, she thought, she would dive back into the archives at the *Post*, but this time the hunt would be for anything related to illegal narcotic activities which connect Denver to Bogotá.

Sleep did eventually arrive, but only after her laptop ran out of battery power. She awoke exhausted, but grateful all the same for at least a couple of nightmare free hours of sleep. Carolina rolled out of bed, threw herself together then ambled off to the *Post*.

All day she scrolled and read, scrolled and read, but came up with nothing. Well, almost nothing that drew any illicit connections between Bogotá, Denver, or the Homeless Coalition. Not even, prior unpaid fishing violations. "Wait a minute, this is interesting," Carolina whispered under her breath. She began reading a biography of Mayor Vargas that she found on Bogotá's website. One brief sentence practically jumped off the page, *Luis Vargas participated in a foreign exchange program his senior year of high school, with a family from Denver Colorado.* "What family? What High School?" These questions immediately flooded her mind. Frustrated by the lack of information, but excited none-the-less by this morsel of information Carolina redirected her search. She found plenty of additional information and biographies on Vargas but no additional information regarding his scholastic exchange.

It was if that information was redacted. She would need to research outside of the web.

"I wonder if Whitten knows about this, too and what is the deal with him not showing me the letter?" she thought to herself. "What kind of sadistic game is this jerk playing? Dead ends, here in the archives. Maybe it's time for this girl to learn how to deep sea fish, I hear they're biting in Bogotá."

CHAPTER 6

Carolina was surprised when she entered Whitten's office and he handed her a boarding pass which he had just printed.

"New editor, new budget," Whitten smiled as he handed her an envelope. "Well C.P., here's your itinerary and company credit card." Carolina's jaw dropped.

"Thank you, sir! I'll go right now and try to get in touch with Mayor Vargas's office to inform him of my arrival and request an interview."

"Remember your assignment is to find the 'Great White Fisherman' of Denver. Interview Mayor Vargas, find out about their relationship, similarities in the two cities and go where the story leads you. And, if can bring up the Homeless Coalition without raising eyebrows then certainly do so. Grab a camera, take pictures!"

"Finally," she thought, "a real assignment!" This once sleep-deprived girl from Indiana was rejuvenated and soaring above the clouds. The rest of the day breezed by and she hurried home. There was no better day than today to visit Karl and the boys. A bell on the door tinkled as it closed behind her. Karl was with a customer, but looked up long enough to acknowledge her with a smile. Carolina patiently sauntered around the store waiting for him to finish. During her perusal something caught her eye, something that for whatever reason she had not observed earlier. There was an old bicycle attached to the wall above the counter. Unlike the others which were lined up in rows throughout the shop, it was apparent this particular bike was significant. There was a bronze plaque with an inscription on the wall directly below, but from where she stood, it was too far away to read. As she strained her eyes to read when a voice from behind her said, "I was never afraid."

Carolina spun around to find one of the bike mechanics looking over her shoulder.

"The inscription reads, *'I was never afraid.'* I have no clue what it means or who wrote it. But just in case you were thinking about asking Mr. Kaleido about that old touring bike, I would advise not to. I almost was fired several years ago for asking him the story behind it. It must be very personal to him. The guys all think it belonged to an old lover who broke his heart. All I know, it's a delicate subject." The mechanic smiled, grabbed a box from a shelf and walked away.

"Well there's a breath of fresh air," Karl's friendly greeting startled Carolina as she watched the departing mechanic and didn't see Karl approach. "Let me see, your rent is not due, so what gives us this honor?"

"Hello sir, the honor is all mine, but I must say a bit overdue. I thought I'd stop in for a visit, but if you're busy, I…"

"Balderdash! I'm never too busy for you," Karl hesitated and furled his lips. "However, I must say that when you come around I don't get much work out of my boys. I see you met Billy," Karl nodded toward the direction his mechanic exited.

Carolina smiled. "He seems nice."

"How are things down at the *Post*? Working on any interesting breaking stories? But, before you answer let me get to my post." Karl put his hand on Carolina's shoulder and directed her to the side while he stepped around and positioned himself behind the counter. "This store is all about appearance, and it needs to appear that someone's minding the store. You never know when a young family might walk through the door looking for new Schwinns for their twins. Karl chuckled. "I could use some sales right now! I'm not selling many bicycles these days, just parts and apparel."

"Maybe you should open a bicycle shop in Bogotá Colombia?" Carolina chimed. But, instead of adding to the levity, Carolina's comment drew a diverse change of expression on Karl's face and tone of his voice.

"What is that supposed to mean?" His sudden awkward mood took her by surprise.

Carolina hesitated for a few seconds before responding, analyzing his retort and giving her time to choose the right response.

"Things are great at the *Post,* I just received my first big assignment. It's complicated and I can't discuss much about it now, but I've been researching Bogotá and have learned they are very committed to promoting bicycles as a preferred mode of transportation. I just thought, well if I said something to disrespect you, I'm very sorry."

Karl nervously cleared his throat then pulled up a chair for her to sit. "You have nothing to apologize for, my dear." The awkward mood continued as his demeanor quickly snapped back. "Congratulations on your promotion!" Yes,

Bogotá has many bicycles. Kaleidospoke's would thrive there." It was pretty apparent that she severed a nerve in Karl. His last sentence trailed off with a sorrowful tone. Carolina glanced up at the bike on the wall and back at Karl, who was distantly staring out the window. And, as much as she wanted to ask, she refrained.

"Well, Karl I'm off to my room," Carolina smiled stepping forward and touching him on the shoulder. He quickly thrust his head around and with a feeble smile said, "Goodnight Rebecca."

Carolina quickly dismissed Karl's farewell, as it was apparent that emotionally he was quite a distance away. She could only surmise where his mind was, but knew at this moment, whoever this Rebecca is, right now she had a torrid grip on Karl.

CHAPTER 7

*F*rom the office of Mayor, Louis Francisco Vargas, Carolina was thrilled to receive this reply, but reading past the heading, the body of the email was not what she wanted to read. "Dear Ms Paige, I regret to inform you that Mayor Vargas will be unavailable during your visit, however in his stead he has offered me, his loyal administrative assistant to be at your beck and call. Our glorious city will open their arms with total hospitality and celebrate your arrival. Cordially, Diego Morales, assistant to the Mayor.

Nevertheless, Carolina was packed and ready to go. "Bogotá here I come!" She muttered as the intercom at Denver International announced the boarding of the jet. Soon she was airborne, her ear buds secure and pillow in place. As the jet ascended in altitude Carolina descended in consciousness.

As the curtain of clouds parted from beyond her window, an image of a lanky women kneeling over an inverted bike on a hot desolate desert road came into focus. The apparent heat of the sun beating down on the back of her neck accompanied with melting tar vapors rising from the asphalt was obviously affecting her by the way she swayed back and forth. Lethargically, the women tugged at the inner tube trying to free it from the belly of the narrow tire. Her motions exemplified her exhaustion, she stopped after each pull to gasp and clutch her abdomen. Helplessly, Carolina could only watch. It was all the women could do to gather enough strength for one last pull. With one hand on the frame of the bike and the other on the black rubber tube, she mustered another yank. Like a rubber band that's stretched beyond its capacity finally snapping and releasing all its energy, so did the tube. Her hand still clutching the tube flailed past her ear twirling her body around which pulled the other hand from its grip on the frame. As her body lunged her hand inadvertently brushed the spokes of the wheel causing it to spin wildly. Physics took over and the women left her feet, flying back and landing her on the ground, the resulting energy snapping her head against the pavement.

Carolina's screech not only woke herself but the man napping in the seat beside her. It also caused heads to turn from the neighboring rows. As a reaction, she immediately looked out the window but there was no image. Relieved, she realized it was only another dream.

An announcement by the captain, instructions by the flight attendant, quick prayer from Carolina, and the slight jolt of the 757 confirmed she was now in Colombia.

Carolina was beaming from ear to ear. She kept repeating under her breath, *"Don't act like a tourist, act professional! Act professional!,* but she was losing the battle, even using the power of suggestion. It was very difficult for her to stifle her emotions, after all it was only the third time she had ever flown and the first time to a new country.

Bogota, the capital and largest city in Colombia, is a city somewhere between a drug-war-battlefield and a hip bohemian city, this phrase, she read a few days ago was now running through Carolina's head as she waited for her luggage at the carousel.

Carolina felt a tap on her shoulder from behind. "Pardon me Senorita. Are you, Carolina Paige of the *Denver Post?*"

"I am," She replied.

Before her stood a dark complexioned man dressed in a tan suit. He was medium in stature and very thin. But, when she acknowledged her name, a warm, tooth-filled, Colombian smile formed from ear to ear.

"My name is Diego Morales, assistant and secretary to Mayor Luis Francisco Vargas and I am at your service. But first, I would like to apologize for my rudeness. I intended to meet you at the gate, but was delayed by unpleasant matters outside of my control. I think you Americans call it 'rush-hour traffic.'"

"So, without any further delay, on behalf of Mayor Francisco Vargas and the fine citizens of Bogotá, Colombia, let me welcome you to our fine city." Diego turned and signaled a large man standing off to the side. He quickly approached and grabbed Carolina's bags. Carolina and Diego followed close behind the large man to a black Mercedes waiting at the curb. Diego opened the backseat door and Carolina entered. He then walked around joining her from the driver's side. The trunk slammed, the driver entered and they were on their way.

"Senorita, where have you made arrangements to stay?"

"Call me Carolina, Diego." Carolina graciously smiled. "I have reservations at the Hilton. May I call you Diego?"

"Yes of course Senorita Paige, I mean Carolina," Diego responded methodically, closely observing how this young American responded.

"So, Diego, where does Mayor Higgins generally stay? I assume, you've picked him up numerous times."

Diego turned to Carolina looking a bit puzzled, "My apology Carolina, I do not know of this Mayor Higgs, of which you inquire."

"It's Higgins and he's the Mayor of Denver, Colorado." Carolina's mouth opened in disbelief to what she was hearing. Diego was now shaking his head. "I am of the understanding that he comes down regularly to go deep sea fishing with Mayor Vargas."

"There must be some mistake. Senor Vargas cannot swim and is deeply terrified of being at sea, especially in a small vessel," Diego emphatically replied.

As the car pulled in front of the Hilton, Diego continued, "Fifty-one weeks of the year, I know every detail of Mayor Vargas schedule, who he sees, when and where he meets and so on. If there was ever a rendezvous between Mayors Vargas and Higgins, I would certainly be aware of it." Diego smiled cordially as he exited the car. He arrived at Carolina's side at the same time as the bellman, but stood back allowing him to open her door. As she stepped out, she looked at Diego and responded.

"So, you said fifty-one weeks. What happens the other week?"

"Why that would be this week, Senorita and well, that's when it becomes none of our business."

Diego nodded at the bellman signaling him to grab her bags, then reached out taking Carolina's hand and delivered her customary kiss to the back. She started toward the lobby, but stopped and turned. "So, Diego will I see you tomorrow?"

"Bright and early, Senorita Paige! Pardon me, Carolina." Diego smiled and gave a deep theatrical bow before climbing into the car.

"The plot thickens." She thought to herself, watching the limo exit the property and merge into the bicycle-littered street.

Carolina was exhausted from the long trip. She tipped the bellman, ordered room service, and then collapsed on her bed. "How wonderful a hot bath would feel," she mused, but quickly dismissed that thought. She fell quickly asleep and to her surprise, she enjoyed an uninterrupted slumber.

CHAPTER 8

There was a tap at the door and waiting on the other side was a silver tray with a long stemmed rose, accompanied with avocados, cayeye, (a traditional Colombian food of cooked green bananas) and of course a silver pot of Colombian coffee. Carolina leaned over and retrieved a note from the tray, "Compliments of Diego Morales. P.S., After you eat and at your leisure, I will be waiting downstairs to show you our beautiful city. Casual/comfortable attire, with no heels," Carolina smiled, then picked up the tray and walked onto on the terrace adjoining her room to enjoy her breakfast. Already this morning she could hear the bustle of the busy street below, which reminded her that she was not there on vacation but at work. She sent her parents and Whitten emails announcing her safe arrival, and then went to work preparing a list of questions for Diego. She quickly finished her breakfast, showered and got ready, then headed down to the lobby. She really didn't have time for a tour of Bogotá, but figured at least she would have a captive audience with Diego, to conduct her interview.

Just as his note declared, Diego indeed was waiting, but Carolina didn't immediately recognize him, in fact, she would have walked past him, if he had not spoken first. Diego's attire was vastly different from the day before. Different indeed! More like awkward. "Spandex! A good journalist doesn't judge," this noble thought rushed to her mind, but quickly faded. After her initial body scan, Carolina forced herself not to drop her eyes below his shoulders.

"Senorita Carolina, you look lovely!"

"Thank you, Diego, and thank you for the delicious breakfast. That was a very nice surprise."

Diego smiled and nodded at Carolina, and then directed her toward the exit and the supposed awaiting car. But the long black limousine from yesterday was not waiting by the curb. In its place was a tandem bicycle.

"I guess that explains the man tights," She thought.

"In Bogotá there's only one way to properly view our city and it's from a bicycle. But, not to worry Carolina, I will do most of the pedaling; you just hold on and enjoy the sights." Diego handed Carolina a helmet and she reluctantly boarded the aft seat of the bike, and within seconds they were on their way.

Her feelings of anxiety only increased as they entered into the street, which was virtually a river of flowing bicycles, mopeds and cars. Carolina's knuckles were bright white from her death grip on the rear handlebars and her face was a near-death shade of pale. She prayed profusely, but interrupted herself often with short bursts of terrorized screams.

Diego was un-phased by his panicking passenger. He calmly kept narrating his guided tour while weaving in and out of traffic. His spiel would have made the Bogotá City Fathers proud. "PLEASE, Can we stop? There's a beautiful cathedral," Carolina screamed in Diego's ear. Diego obliged and pedaled onto the sidewalk alongside the massive facade. Carolina wasted no time dismounting before she had her helmet removed and hair straightened.

Diego too was off the bike and continuing his shtick. "I see Senorita, you like so many visitors daily are called to this beautiful architectural masterpiece." I behold to you 'Iglesia-de-Francisco', translated, the Church of San Francisco! This beautiful sacred house of worship was built in the mid fifteen hundreds. The chapels were actually constructed on ships before moving them to shore and then into place. In 1743 and again in 1785 the building was severely damaged by earthquakes, but by the grace of God, survived, to be the oldest church in Bogotá. Would you like to see inside?"

"Yes, I would love!" Carolina responded in an anxious, yet deliberate voice. Diego was partially correct. Even though Carolina wished that the chilling bike ride would conclude, she did feel invited by the magnificence of this ancient church. Perhaps she was drawn to it, like a sailor finding consolation in spotting a lighthouse in a stormy sea. Nevertheless, now that her feet were safely touching the ground, she felt compelled to go inside. But, not before shooting several pictures of the facade with her newly acquired *Post* camera.

Carolina followed Diego through the mammoth wood doors into a foyer, which connected a series of long corridors running in many directions. Diego stopped as if to prepare to receive a volley of questions from Carolina, but she instead, stepped around and began hastily walking down one of the marbled halls. She appeared to know exactly where she was going. Her eyes were fixed, staring up at the high arched ceiling of painted murals and walls of century old tapestries. Diego caught up, but instinct told him to say nothing. In reverence, he backed off a few steps, giving her space to reflect.

Diego had walked this corridor a thousand times in his life, but this time his focus was not on the religious mosaics and tapestries, but rather his mesmerized guest. At the end of the corridor was a large doorway, the main entrance to the massive lavish gold cathedral. The room was even more breathtaking than the corridor which lent entry. When Carolina arrived at the door, she stopped and her mouth fell opened in wonder.

"Diego, this is the most beautiful place that I have ever seen!" She was truly moved. With misty eyes, she turned around and looked at her host, who had just caught up to hear her affirmation.

"Please, can we sit for a while?"

"Of course, Senorita!"

Diego attentively, took her arm and they walked down the aisle to a random pew near the alter. The cathedral was virtually empty with the exception of a young woman kneeling about midway down the aisle. When they walked past her, the girl looked up as if she were preparing to speak, but then looked away. Carolina hesitated, feeling a strange sensation, as if she recognized this girl, but Diego tugged at her and they continued to their seats.

"Are you all right, Carolina? You look like you've seen a ghost. I can call a car and return you to the hotel."

"Diego, I am so sorry, I just need a few moments to gather myself. I don't know what came over me." Carolina wiped her eyes and continued looking. After a few minutes, she finally spoke, whispering to Diego, "I must say, that I was terrified by our short bicycle ride." She looked at Diego and smiled. "Pretty silly, right? I don't know how you navigate through all of the traffic without becoming a statistic. However, the most amazing thing happened. When I entered the doors of this church, my lingering feelings of duress from the ride were gone. It's embarrassing to admit, but I really can't describe my feelings. It wasn't, a premonition, or even an epiphany, it was as if someone was waiting for me here and that 'someone' was pulling me into the cathedral. But the only other person here is that young girl who smiled as we passed beside her pew." Diego looked puzzled, "What young girl? There is no one else here, we are alone." Simultaneously, they both twisted around to view rows of empty pews.

Carolina stood and pointed in the direct to where she sat. "You did not see her? Well; I guess she must have gone." Carolina glanced around the room and then down at Diego and sat back down. "Diego, I really appreciate you taking time to show me around Bogotá and I do want to hear more about this church, as well as the rest of your historical city. I do need to ask you a few other non-tourist-like questions too."

"You were not specific in your letter of what you wanted to interview Mayor Vargas, but most who come here from the United States normally wish to discuss vacation destinations, so I assumed," Diego looked attentively at Carolina.

"Diego, Denver's mayor, Arthur Higgins vacations quite often in Bogotá. In fact he is supposedly down here now, ironically the same week that your Mayor Vargas is out of commission. I was led to believe that they were fishing buddies. My intent was to write an article about their relationship, how it got started, and their parallels of running major cities, their love of fishing, that sort of thing. So, your revelation that these two prestigious gentlemen have never met changes my entire storyline." Carolina's mind raced as she pieced together her thoughts, before speaking, "A very mysterious twist of events, don't you think?"

"Oh Carolina, you mustn't take the fact that I know nothing of their relationship and turn it into something perhaps that it's not. I'm sure there's a simple explanation."

"Diego, yesterday you were pretty adamant that these gentlemen never met. Are you now wavering in your opinion?"

"No Senorita, I only tell you what I know."

CHAPTER 9

"Diego, I really do need to ask Mayor Vargas just a few questions. Is there any way that you can arrange this while I am here?"

"A meeting with Mayor Vargas will not be possible this week," Diego stated.

Perhaps if I extend my stay, you can arrange a short meeting when he returns," pleaded Carolina.

"He is a very busy man; so I cannot make certain the length of your interview." Carolina's determined appeal to Diego was causing him to waver in his position.

"Thank you Diego! I will change my itinerary to extend my stay. I know he is a very busy, but all I need is fifteen minutes. I'll keep my questions short and concise."

"However, you my friend can help me with some of my questions now," Carolina continues. "In your perspective, how was Mayor Vargas able to convert Bogotá from a very violent, high crime, drug cartel controlled city into a thriving and vibrant modern urban oasis?" To reward Diego for his promise of a meeting with Vargas, she without interruption let him do what he was so very well-groomed to do, pompously bloviate on the accomplishments of his city. After several minutes of letting him go on his own, she craftily began steering the conversation to expand specifically on the drug cartels, who they were and how they operated and his answer wasn't what she expected.

"You don't understand, we were all the drug cartels! Every family, every citizen had some sort of involvement. Not all were involved in the darker side of enforcement, but we were manufacturers, distributors, marketers, enablers. It was our economy, our livelihood and it was our demon too. It was eating us alive."

"So much killing! So much senseless killing of others, so much senseless killing of our own families, and all over greed." Diego's voice cracked and he looked away. "Saint Peter, have mercy on our souls!"

After a few moments of silence, Carolina asked him another question, changing to a lighter subject.

"How long have you worked for Mayor Vargas?"

"Since I was twelve years old, long before he was mayor. My sister and I washed dishes and worked the garden. My Mother was their housekeeper; I practically grew up in the Vargas home. He took very good care of my sister, mother and me after my father died in the Cartel Wars. Our family is very indebted to Senor Vargas and his family!"

"You are very loyal, Diego. I thought that I would ask Mayor Vargas about his studies in the United States. Are you familiar with any of the details?"

"Actually, that subject, I am not." Diego stopped to think, then shook his head, "I know vaguely about this. He rarely reminisces of his youth."

"So that you know, I also plan on asking him if he's ever met Denver's mayor Higgins and depending on his answer, it will determine the direction of my follow up questions. It might even include a question of how he spent his prior week. You know, that mysterious *one week of the year*?" Carolina deliberately phrased this dig to get his reaction. She started sensing that Diego knew exactly where his boss was and what he was doing. Diego didn't hesitate with his response. "Don't even consider asking that follow-up question! If he says he's never met your mayor, then let it go, or your meeting will conclude at that point!" Diego's tone sharply turned.

Carolina stuck out her hand and said, "That's fair. Deal!" Diego looked her in the eye and a few moments later broke a smile, and then shook her hand.

"Deal!"

"By the way, Diego, how far is the coast from here, perhaps the nearest fishing marina? And, how would one normally get there."

"The nearest fishing port is Buenaventure and it's over the Andes Mountains. Driving by car is a long ten to twelve hours and sometimes a dangerous journey. But, I know why you ask, trust me, there is no way Mayor Vargas would fly there without my knowledge."

"So, could you arrange a flight for me?"

Agitated, Diego looked at Carolina in disbelief. She continued, "I know, Diego. Didn't I just hear a word that you said?" Carolina smiled. "Now what kind of a journalist would I be if I didn't chase down every lead?"

"Of course I can Senorita. I'll arrange a flight for us in the morning."

"No, Diego! As much as I enjoy your company, I cannot burden you with chaperoning me around Colombia. Flying me to Buenaventure is too much of an imposition. I just need to know where I make the arrangements and do they accept credit cards?"

"That is exactly why I need to travel with you to Buenaventure!" Diego, laughed. "Your 'credit card' will only be useful to open locked doors in most places here in Colombia. If you try to make a transaction and all you have is a thin piece of plastic you will most likely be dragged out of town and beaten and that's if you're lucky. Unfortunately venturing alone anywhere outside of the tourist areas of Bogotá is not a wise decision.

"Carolina, I assure you that it is not a burden to accompany a beautiful woman such as yourself, regardless of where she wishes to go in Colombia. I insist, it would be my pleasure!"

"But, we still have plenty of daylight left in this day; shall we continue our excursion around Bogotá? I'll summon a car for the remainder of the day."

"That my friend will not be necessary. You delivered me safely here and I'm over the fear, so let's ride!" Carolina jumped up, followed by Diego. They retraced their steps up the aisle. Carolina hesitated at the row where the young girl knelt, looked around and then proceeded to the exit.

Conscious of her fears, Diego rerouted his tour to less heavily-traveled streets for the rest of their excursion.

"I will make the arrangements for our day flight to Buenaventure and send a car for you in the morning," Diego instructed Carolina as she dismounted the bicycle in front of the hotel.

"Gracias, my friend! I will see you in the morning."

CHAPTER 10

Carolina hurriedly rushed to her room, as she needed to Skype Whitten at their prearranged time. It was crucial. She needed to inform him of her intentions of staying another week in order to interview Mayor Vargas. But when she arrived at her room, all of her prior intensions were vanquished by what appeared to be an unwanted visitor. She had been robbed! She took two steps into her room, and then bolted back into the hall. Leaving her door wide open, she ran to the elevator. She anxiously summoned security and the manager from the front desk and within minutes the entourage escorted her to her room.

Her clothes were strewn all over the room. The sheets were pulled off the bed and down to the bare mattress. Carolina pushed her way around a security cop and rushed to the bathroom closet only to find her room safe gapping wide open. Jump drives, voice recorder, reserve cash and more significantly her passport were all gone. When she turned around, on the mirror above the sink was a glaring message written brazenly with her red lipstick,

"VOLVER A CASA O CONJ MORIRDE!"

She frantically turned and darted toward the nightstand, only to find that her laptop was missing too. With her hands over her mouth and fighting back tears, she pirouetted once then fell into the chair next to the bed.

The manager quickly approached her. "Not to worry Senorita Paige, we will get those who are responsible for this and hopefully get your belongings returned. The Bogotá Police have been notified and they will be here shortly. There are multiple security cameras in the halls and at multiple locations including all exists. There is no way they could have escaped without us knowing what they look like."

"Once the police conduct their questioning and all the reports are filled out, we will get you a new room. Is there anything I can get you while we wait?" Before Carolina had a chance to respond to the manager, two policemen came through the door. Suddenly, her room was bulging with humanity, three hotel security officers, two Bogotá policemen, the hotel manager and a woman from hotel housekeeping.

A salvo of Spanish filled the air. Despite Carolina's two semesters of college Spanish, she was not able to keep up with her comprehension of the fluid flourish of linguistics. She reached out and grabbed the arm of the manager to get his attention.

"Sir, there is something you can do for me. I am going to need a computer and secure access to the internet. I'm having trouble getting service here on my iPhone." There was nothing wrong with Carolina's phone, but she was cautious in case someone was listened.

"Yes, but of course. You may use one of our computers in our office."

They both looked up as one of the police officers approached with his clipboard. The hotel manager smiled and graciously excused himself. In broken English the officer introduced himself to Carolina, and then began interrogating her in a tone that was normally inappropriate for the victim of a crime. He handed her the clipboard and instructed her to print her pertinent information such as name, address, occupation. He stood within inches of her chair watching every scroll of her pen. Carolina finished filling out the form and handed back his clipboard. The officer read what she wrote and then verbally asked her for the same information again to see if she responded the same. When he was satisfied with whom she said she was and only after thoroughly examining her driver's license, he finished his line of questioning.

During his routine, he kept eyeing her bed, as if to hint he would like to sit. Finally Carolina could not overlook the obvious and obliged by gesturing toward the bed with her hand. The officer sat down immediately nearly sitting on her camera which she had laid there a few minutes earlier. Now he was comfortable on his new perch, but he did not relax in his questioning. "Senorita Paige, I am perplexed. Would you help me understand one question which I'm struggling with? Why would a young girl, such as you travel alone to Bogotá? Do you know anyone here?"

Carolina glared at him for several seconds before responding, and then she leaned over and with her index finger thumped his clipboard. "I am Carolina Paige, investigative journalist for the *Denver Post*, Denver, Colorado, United States of America. I am here doing a newspaper article on Bogotá and I have just spent the day with Diego Morales, assistant to Mayor Luis Vargas."

The officer looked at the camera and immediately his demeanor changed. In fact he jumped up from the bed and looked over at the other officer, who then hurriedly exited the room. He then looked back at Carolina. "Tell me Senorita, do you understand the message that was left for you on your mirror?"

"Something about home?" Carolina shook her head. "My Spanish is not so good."

"Let me help you with the translation. The message left by your guest or guests, 'Go home or die'!"

"Why would thieves leave you such a message? The thing is Senorita, we may have a lot of crime here in Bogotá, but the Bogotá Hilton with its high security is rarely a target. As far as we know at this time, your room was the only room in this grand hotel to be broke into. In fact, it has been several years since we've experienced a break-in here. So, surely you must understand my bewilderment?"

Just then the other officer entered back into the room and summonsed his superior into the hall. After what seemed an eternity for Carolina, they returned.

"Well Senorita, your story checks out. In fact, Senor Morales has requested special police security for you for the rest of your stay. Hotel security is in the process of reviewing the security video. They report that it appears there were two male individuals wearing facemasks and hotel staff jackets. They were pushing a maid cart which they took into the room. When they departed, they nearly ran over a young woman with a bike standing outside of your door. For some reason the footage at that point became very grainy. We are working on identifying this woman, finding her could be crucial."

"Was she Colombian?" Carolina excitedly asked.

"I'm not sure. They didn't say. Does this description match someone you know?"

"No, I guess not, I'm not sure why I asked." Carolina, recalled the young girl in church to be light-skinned with short light brown hair. She also thought she looked like the cyclist in her dream, but quickly dismissed that notion, as crazy.

The hotel manager politely approached. "Pardon me Officer, but if your interview is complete with Senorita Paige, I would like to show her to her new room."

"Yes, we are complete as of now. You may show our American friend her room." The officer smiled and bowed in respect. "There will be a guard at all times in front of your door as well as the lobby. Senor Morales passed on his regrets and said that he will see you at eight a.m. in the lobby. Once again, I am very sorry for your inconvenience."

Carolina guardedly smiled at him then began gathering her belongings and stuffing them into her luggage. With that, the officer in charge along with the hotel security guards exited the room. Carolina had been feeling her phone vibrating for some time, but had not taken the time to view it until now. There were several unread emails, three missed calls, two from Whitten and one from her landlord, Karl Kaleido. She looked around the room to make sure that she had collected all of her possessions, and then turned to the manger.

He noticed her viewing her phone and anticipated her next request. "Would you like me to take you to a secure phone and computer now? My staff will deliver your bags to your room."

Without hesitation, Carolina responded, "Yes, please."

He escorted her to the main floor and to a room, which he opened with a swipe of his plastic key. The office wasn't much larger than a closet, but it had a desk, a computer and a land phone. It was perfect.

"Here you are, Senorita. Use it as long as you wish and when you are done, come get me. I will be at the front desk."

She thanked him and he closed the door behind her Carolina immediately called Whitten. His phone only rang once before he answered, "CAROLINA!"

"Yes, boss."

"Thank God, you're okay!" The anxiety and pitch of Whitten's voice was not anticipated, after all she was the one trying to keep her composure.

"Boss, my room was broken into and my passport was stolen. There was a threat on my life. But I'm okay."

"Listen Carolina, I made a huge mistake by letting you go alone on this assignment. This story is much larger than I thought, not only larger, but dangerous. My house was broken into as well and I've been receiving death threats. Your landlord called and your apartment was ransacked. Your life may be in danger. You must immediately go to the American Embassy and tell them what's going on. They can get you a temporary passport and make arrangements for your security, until you can make the next flight out of there."

"Boss, the Bogotá Police with orders from the Mayor's office has issued special security for me. I'll be fine. Tomorrow I'm going to accompany the Mayor's assistant to the fishing town of Buenaventura. Hopefully I'll locate Mayor Higgins. Please, I'm just getting started!"

"Carolina, you don't understand. That mysterious letter that I had recieved was from Mayor Vargas's office. Even though it was unsigned, whoever sent it had access to the Bogotá mayor's stationary and insignia. They were deliberate in using this official parchment to reinforce their message and expel any notion that it was a hoax. The letter told me to 'follow the money to Denver's Homeless Coalition; it would lead to the truth.' Carolina, the letter also enclosed an old Polaroid photo of two teenage boys. Inscribed on the back were the names Luis and Arthur, 'Brothers from a different country,' 1966.'

"Get your ass to the Embassy, then on a plane out of there! Please!" Whitten, hesitated to hear her reply, which never came, so he hung up.

CHAPTER 11

"I need to call Karl," Was the only thought racing through Carolina's mind. She wasn't about to come home until she had her story. Her first emotion of fear was now replaced with anger over the invasion of her privacy and the cowardly threats.

She picked up the phone and called Kaleidospokes, but Karl wasn't there, so she left a message with the employee who answered. "Tell Karl that I am fine and still in Colombia. Tell him that I got the message from my boss regarding the break-in and that I will see him in a few days."

Carolina typed a quick report and emailed it to Whitten. Leaving the office, she looked for the manager. She needed to go to the Embassy and was hoping that he could accommodate her with transportation.

The hotel was more than happy to grant her request. They provided her with a car and driver. As a U.S. citizen she definitely needed to report the crime and apply for a temporary passport. Her business at the American Embassy went quick and they were very efficient, however getting a temporary passport would take a few days. That's all she needed to hear. Carolina didn't completely ignore Whitten; it was just the timing of her departure with which she took liberty. She couldn't fly until she had a passport, so there was no point in contacting the airline until all her paperwork was in hand. "I surely wouldn't get in trouble over schematics," She thought.

When she returned to the hotel, she was greeted by her new best friend, one of Bogotá's finest. The police officer opened the car door then escorted her all the way to her new room. Carolina felt like a rock star, but most of all she felt safe, at least for the moment. He took his position on a wooden chair outside of her door and remained there for the rest of the night.

Carolina no more than closed her door and her phone rang. It was Diego. He called to personally check on her and to offer his assistance with anything that she may need. Of course, he wished to convey the following official statement, "As a representative of the highest office in

Bogotá, and on behalf of Mayor Vargas, we are extremely embarrassed that a guest of our city would be treated so poorly. I assure you that our police department is doing everything they can possibly do to catch the thieves responsible for this crime and to return your stolen items."

She thanked him for checking on her and for assigning a guard to stand watch. Diego was expecting her to cancel their trip to Buenaventure and was surprised to hear her enthusiasm about going. Their call concluded with both wishing the other a cordial goodnight.

Carolina fell asleep watching a rerun of the *Bob Newhart Show*, in Spanish on Television.

She fell into a deep sleep, but was awakened hours later by a loud knock at the door. When she opened it she was expecting to see the guard, but a Colombian Policeman it was not! The door frame was filled with a foggy haze except for the outline of a young girl about three or four feet tall. It was not just a girl; it was *the girl*, the same troubled girl who haunted her dreams repeatedly in Denver. She looked up at Carolina; her arms were concealed behind her back until Carolina leaned forward. Then a big grin formed on her face as she brought her arm around and opened her clinched fist, exposing a tootsie roll candy. Carolina gasped! She momentarily took her eyes off the little girl, to peer outside of her door only to find the guard slumped over in his chair. Beside the chair and on the floor sat a discarded brown pint. She quickly turned back to the little girl who was backing away from the door. She stopped and pointed down the hall, then motioned for Carolina to follow.

"Sweetheart, why are you here? What do you want? Please talk to me." Carolina pleaded for some oral response, but the child said nothing. She just continued to walk and motion Carolina to follow.

So, Carolina began to follow. She walked into the hall, passing unnoticed by the unconscious guard, but the closer she got to the child, the faster she walked. She was now running and darted though the exit door next to the elevator. Carolina began running too chasing after this little girl. When she arrived at the exit, she extended her arm, grabbed the knob and pushed. The door flung open.

Carolina stopped dead in her tracks. On the other side of the door was not the stairwell, it was a street. A few feet away was not the little girl, but a woman on a bicycle preparing to pedal away. The slamming of the door caused her to stop and turn. She looked directly at Carolina. Despite the darkness and the fog, Carolina instantly recognized her face. It was the young woman from Iglesia-de-Francisco and now apparent to Carolina, this was the same women she saw fixing her tire in the desert.

Suddenly, two blinding bright lights appeared and they were heading toward her! A car barreled directly toward the cyclist, she turned around, but it was too late. Carolina's scream didn't drown out the sound of the hideous dull thud. Her instantaneous reaction was to clinch, turn her head and close her eyes.

"Senorita Paige! Senorita Paige! Are you okay?"

"OH GOD," Screamed Carolina! Her eye lids flew open and her fully dilated pupils were inches from the body guard hovering over her. She sat up and looked around, then looked back at the guard.

"Where am I?"

"Senorita, you are just inside the salida. You came out of your room and ran toward this puerta. I yelled, but you did not stop. You were through the puerta, before I could catch up. I found you on the landing before the steps. Are you alright? Shall I summon a medico?"

"I'm okay, gracias." Carolina took a moment to gather her thoughts before continuing. "Did you see a little girl or perhaps a young senorita with a bicicleta?" He looked at Carolina as if he were having trouble with what she was asking, then shook his head.

"No comprende."

Carolina tried again needing to validate what was real from what was a dream.

"Was there anyone else in the hall besides me?"

"No Senorita! It was only you. Let me get you back to your room."

Carolina reached out and grabbed his hand and he pulled her to her feet. He walked her back to her room where she spent another sleepless night.

CHAPTER 12

Diego was waiting in the lobby as he said he would, this time not sporting spandex, but rather some sort of khaki sportsman's outfit, complete with a Bombay hat decorated with fishing lures. The elevator opened and Carolina walked out with her police guard.

"Good morning, my new American friend, even though I understand that your troubles continued into the night. I hope that you were able to get some sleep."

"Hello, Diego. That is you, right? I wasn't sure if it was you or perhaps Papa Hemingway." Carolina smiled as she looked him over.

"American humor, right Carolina?"

"Not really, my friend, just sarcasm by a sleepless bitch. My apologies Diego, one cup of your amazing county's coffee and I will be nice as new!"

Diego had her coffee waiting in the limo and before she stirred in her sugar they were at the airport. The driver drove through a two gates, then directly onto the tarmac where a twin engine plane was warming up. Carolina, Diego and the body guard exited the car, they directly boarded the plane, taxied and were soon in the air. Even though the flight was relatively short in duration, it wasn't exactly pleasant. The updrafts from the wind current over the Andes made for a very bumpy flight. Luckily before airsickness bags were deployed they were on the ground in a small airfield near Buenaventura.

The airport consisted of a military style Quonset hut used for a terminal and a large rusted tin hangar with part of the roof missing. Littered around the buildings were skeletons of airplanes and several pallets heaped with parts, but no other signs of humanity. There was only one runway leading to a crack-riddled, weed-infested, concrete tarmac. Waiting in the middle of the tarmac of this seemingly abandoned airfield was a taxi van.

Diego shouted instructions to the pilot over the low buzz of the propellers, while Carolina and her guard climbed out of the plane and into the taxi. A few moments later Diego joined them. As the car pulled away, the airplane departed.

"Not to worry, Senorita. He will return this afternoon," Diego smiled.

The ride from the airfield to Buenaventura took approximately twenty minutes and then another twenty minutes through town to the harbor. The busy narrow streets were much like Bogotá, but a lot less touristy. There was a real sense of bustling, a purposeful frenzy of trucks and vans rushing commodities from the docked ships to the warehouses or stores. Bicycles appeared to be used for delivery, not pleasure.

From the window of the taxi, Carolina witnessed a surreal image of great despair in stark contrast to the bustling commerce of the tourist district in Bogotá. Poor and desperate people walked, stood or sat along the roadside. These people covered all demographics from the very young to the very old-young mothers holding crying babies, children in rags, crippled and afflicted. people with sorrowful eyes. Carolina had never witnessed such despair in her life, and it was hard for her to look, but she pointed her camera and pressed, capturing poignant photo images.

"Their eyes are all so far away. Diego, why are they gathering here, are they waiting for assistance or aid?"

"There is no one to assist them. No government programs. No Homeless Coalition, like you have in your city of Denver," Diego opined.

Carolina was surprised by his remark. She looked away from the human plight and inquisitively at Diego.

"So, you know about Denver's Homeless Coalition? I'm impressed!"

Diego seemed angered, and immediately looked away. "I do my research."

"Very sad," Carolina uttered quietly.

"Diego, can you take me around the docks and introduce me to some fishing boat captains? It's probably a long shot, but maybe I'll luck out and find a captain who knows Mayor Higgins."

"Si," Diego, nodded at Carolina.

Diego leaned forward and gave instructions to both the driver and the guard sitting next to him in the passenger seat. The car turned down a very narrow alley, a passageway between two, four story apartment dwellings. When they emerged, they were at the docks. Suddenly they were on a very wide concrete paved platform, approximately thirty meters in width. It was perpendicular to the alley and buildings and parallel to the ocean. Despite large freighters blocking the view of the water, Carolina's other senses came alive. She could smell and taste the sea. Seabirds dipped and dived among the pedestrian traffic, scavenging whatever they could. The taxi crept forward until it was mired in traffic, then it stopped. The driver and Diego exchanged a few words, then all three got out.

"From here we walk," Diego took the lead, then Carolina, followed by the police bodyguard. Once they passed the large freighters and commercial fishing trawlers, the traffic thinned. They walked for about five city blocks to where the docks narrowed and jetties extended out.

"The jetties dock smaller boats of all types, but mostly sport fishing. If your mayor came to Buenaventura to sportfish, this is where he would come. Some of the boats are most likely out to sea, but there is always a representative who remains to set up charters. Shall we?" Diego gestured to Carolina for her approval and she responded by leading the way down the first jetty.

The jetties were like walking through the midway of a carnival or a county fair in the States. Nearly every dock had its own banners or signs at the front of the dock advertising their charters. Adjacent to the banners stood young charismatic locals, sporting smiles and handing out flyers. It was a potpourri of water sports, from sunset cruises to sailing, and of course deep sea fishing. But according to one young salesperson, even if you didn't see what you wanted, just ask and they would accommodate. Diego guided the three of them through the minutia and deliberately toward a tall boat with outriggers.

"Buenas dias!" An old man sitting on a gang box in front of the boat greeted the approaching group.

"Hola!" Diego replied.

"Would you like to go fishing? We catch the biggest fish in all of Colombia!" The man stood up and smiled, exposing a few missing teeth. "And, as you can hear, I speak perfect English too." The man laughed.

"Not today, Anciano. My American friend has a few questions that she would like to ask you."

The old man nodded as if he understood, then looked at Carolina. After the quick introduction, Carolina stepped forward and Diego and the guard backed away.

"We'll be waiting for you, back on the dock. No Hurry." Diego told Carolina, and then the two men walked away. Carolina approached the man, respectful of his space, but getting close enough so that she could show him a photo of Mayor Higgins on her phone.

"Hi, my name is Carolina Paige. I am a journalist for a Colorado, USA newspaper and I am…"

"Looking for my Mayor!" A loud voice came bellowing up from the boat, finishing her sentence.

Carolina turned around to see a lanky man in a dirty white tee-shirt and blue cap exiting the boat. He was clenching down on an unlit cigar, but took it out of his mouth to spit, before he spoke. "Vamos!" The old man grimaced after receiving his order, then walked away.

"So, what kind of man be it mayor or not, lets a beautiful journalist chase after him, all the way to another continent, but doesn't let her catch him? That confuses my mind!" He laughed, wiped his hand across his shirt, reached out, took her hand and kissed it. "My name is Captain Jorge Herrera, how can I be of service to you?"

"Wow, that's quite an introduction. So what makes you think that I was looking for 'my mayor' or for that matter anyone? What makes you presume I was chasing him, or for that matter, anyone to another continent? Who are you, Captain Herrera, a person that I have never met, presumptuous enough to finish my sentence?" Carolina's reply, let him know that she wasn't about to be intimidated by his surly disposition. It worked. He instantly responded to her retort with a smile, and then nodded in the direction of Diego and the guard.

"Your friend up there visited yesterday, saying that he would bring you by."

"Really? So I can rule out that you aren't some sort of modern day Colombian profiteer."

"Very amusing Senorita Paige!" The captain replied.

"Well, since you already have the advantage on me and apparently have all ready been questioned, or perhaps the word is, prepared, I'll change my intended questions. I am now just very interested in your conversations with Senor Morales," Carolina declared. "Did he ask you if you ever guided Arthur Higgins on a fishing expedition? Or, perhaps instead, tell you to say that you did?" When Carolina finished her sentence, she glanced up to see Diego and his guard intensely staring back at them. When they spotted her looking their way, they urgently began walking down the jetty. Carolina looked back at the captain who also had noticed them and was now grinning from ear to ear.

"I took your mayor out fishing all week. We were very successful catching our limit of fish. The mayor was very happy and said that he would be returning to the United States this morning."

As the Captain was concluding his seemingly prepared statement, Diego and the guard arrived. The captain's posture became rigid with their arrival. He took two steps back, and then placed his hand on the handle of his knife, which was securely sheathed on his belt. Carolina stared perplexed at the captain after his coy remark and change in demeanor.

"Carolina, perhaps you have found out some useful information from the good Captain?" Inquired Diego, walking toward her. The atmosphere immediately turned tense, Carolina could sense a dramatic change in the disposition of all three men. Despite Diego specifically addressing her, she couldn't take her eyes off of the captain's defensive body language.

"Yes, uh yes I did, Diego! Captain Herrera here was just telling me that he indeed took Arthur Higgins fishing this week. And, damn the luck, I missed him! He said that the Mayor has already departed, back to America." Carolina never broke her intense glare at the captain. "Isn't that right, Captain Herrera?"

The captain cocked his head a bit and nodded, Yes, you understood me correct, that is what happened." The captain was now staring back at Carolina, but his smile had returned, and then he looked toward Diego.

"Was there anything else that I can help you with?"

Diego looked at Carolina, waiting for her to respond.

"No Captain, you've been more than enlightening. Thank you." Carolina turned and began her exit up the jetty to shore. The other two took her lead and fell in close behind her. When Carolina was comfortable that she had Diego and the body guard far enough away from earshot, a few steps from shore, she stopped.

"Oh wait," she abruptly proclaimed. "For my record, I need to get some contact information from the captain. I'm sorry. This will only take a minute." Carolina turned, brushed past her two-man entourage and ran back. Momentarily she arrived back at Captain Herrera's vessel. He was on board tending to his gear, but quickly looked up when she arrived.

"I had a feeling that you were not done with your questions," the Captain laughed and walked over to the edge of the boat, closer to Carolina.

"You never took Mayor Arthur Higgins fishing, did you Captain?"

"Never met the man, in my life." The Captain propped his leg up on the side rail of the boat and looked sternly at Carolina. "But, you're a smart cookie. You didn't need my confirmation to know that."

Carolina nodded, and then started to back away, but the Captain offered her one more bit of parting advice.

"Senorita, be careful. Those two amigos with you, are bad hombres!"

CHAPTER 13

For the ride and flight back to Bogotá, there were very few words spoken. Carolina was perplexed by Diego's prearranged encounter with Captain Herrera. She was also uncomfortable by the Captain's parting advice. Her mind was a swirl of endless scenarios explaining Diego's deceptive theater. But she would at least for now play along with his little charade. She suspected that he may know that she didn't buy his little scam anyway. After all, his sting didn't exactly come off flawlessly.

Finally, on the last leg of the journey, from the plane to her hotel, Diego broke the silence.

"I am disappointed that you did not get to make contact with your mayor. Perhaps better luck next year. Good news. We have been in contact with your American Consulate, and they are expediting your temporary

84

passport. You can hopefully return as early as tomorrow to the United States."

"Oh, but Diego, did you forget about my extended stay in order to interview your Mayor Vargas? My chance encounter with Mayor Higgins was a less significant part of my agenda. After all, I have access to him anytime."

"With all that has happened, like your burglary, I just thought that…"

"Are you kidding me?! If anything it emboldens me! I'm an American! I don't cower, or take orders from common thieves." Carolina took a quick jab at Diego, as the car pulled in front of the hotel.

"Thank you so much for taking me to Buenaventura. I'm sure that you had better things to do than babysit me, not to mention the expense."

"It's been my pleasure, Senorita. While you are in Bogotá, you are my responsibility. You may quote me on this; we are grateful for American tourism which infuses millions of dollars annually into our economy. The truth is, we can't afford to have something unfortunate happen to a visitor from the United States, especially a journalist from a major newspaper. That would be devastating. The expense as you say is a small pittance and only insurance to Bogotá." The car doors opened and Carolina and the body guard exited. "Senorita, I will be in touch," Imparted Diego.

Everywhere that Carolina went her newly assigned shadow was at her side. Her first stop was the hotel office to make her daily secure land line phone call to Whitten. She was able to leave him standing outside the door while she placed the call. The phone only rang once, before Whitten picked up.

"Paige!"

"Yes, Boss."

"Are you safe? How was your day? Tell me something I don't know!" Before Carolina could take a breath, Whitten had fired this barrage of questions at her.

"Yes! Good! And, Mayor Higgins doesn't like to fish," Carolina snickered. "Well, that last bit of info is still speculative." Carolina proceeded to tell him of her day's events, starting after her regaining consciousness on the cold concrete floor of the hotel exit. That information she deemed as private and wasn't prepared to share it with anyone, unless perhaps a shrink. She also made certain to calculate her words carefully while explaining Diego's prearranged visit with the captain at the marina. She knew that Whitten was ready to pull the plug on her stay and would be quick to order her to bug out, even if it meant personally asking the State Department to expedite her temporary passport. But, she came for a story and she wasn't about to leave without one. That was still her mantra. Despite toning down the drama, Whitten suspected that she was stepping on some sensitive toes of dangerous foes by the recent turn of events.

"Listen Paige, I screwed up by letting you go there alone, it's too dangerous. I figured one reporter doing a harmless story on Bogotá wouldn't draw attention, but I was wrong. Have you checked in with the U.S. Embassy like I requested?"

"Yes sir and they are working on getting my temporary passport. It shouldn't take more than a couple of days."

"You lay low and don't leave the Hotel until they contact you with your temporary. Once you have it, you get to the airport and get the hell out of there! Whatever you have so far is good enough. I'll put my back up plan into motion."

"Back up plan?" Inquired Carolina

"I made connections with a Colombian private investigator who claims not to be loyal to this current administration. I've already asked him to do a background check on your friend Diego. When he gets back with me, I'll just ask him to dig a little deeper to see what he can come up with." Their conversation concluded with Carolina feeling very defeated.

She took a minute to organize her thoughts before exiting the office, but when she did her body guard was waiting. Carolina smiled and tapped him on the shoulder and they walked side-by-side across the lobby to the hall of elevators. The guard reached around her and pushed the up button on the wall. When he did Carolina noticed that he was perspiring tremendously. He was also trembling and looked very pale.

The bell chimed as the door opened, but he did not advance forward, or even look up, he just drew a heavy breath.

"Are you okay, amigo?" Concerned about his demeanor, Carolina stepped closer to examine his face, letting the door to the empty elevator close in front of them. Carolina instinctively backed away as soon as she heard him begin to repetitively clear his throat. She recognized the unpleasant sound every human makes right before they involuntarily empty their stomach. Suddenly, his head jerked up and his arm flew wide, pointing her in the direction of a bench. He then cupped his hands over his mouth and sprinted away in the direction of the servicios.

"At least he didn't lose it while we were on the elevator," Carolina muttered, as she reached out to push the button to re-summon the elevator. Before her finger touched the silver button, she turned around to glance at the pillowed bench, where apparently the guard wanted her to wait for his return. Defiantly she shook her head, confirming her rejection of his order, but something appeared in her peripheral vision that made her redirect her thoughts completely.

CHAPTER 14

It was her! Standing in the exit door to the street was the woman with her bike. And, once again she was motioning Carolina to follow. Real or apparition, this female was dressed in a white cotton button shirt and ragged khaki pants. Her motions this time were more deliberate and urgent. When Carolina began walking toward her, she put her leather bicycle helmet on and pushed her bike the rest of the way through the exit.

"Wait!" Carolina shouted. But the door slammed behind the her.

Carolina burst through the door within seconds of the cyclist. The sidewalk was crowded with pedestrians and the street was just as busy. Carolina's head pivoted from side to side, trying to see which direction her recent acquaintance went. "There she goes!" Carolina spotted her a few of hundred meters ahead of her. Once again she looked back and motioned her to follow. Carolina began to chase after her. She ran for blocks and blocks, sometimes on the sidewalk, other times on the street. Wherever she could visually see the female cyclist and dodge pedestrians she stayed on course. In her mind she was processing this bizarre data, "Was she dreaming again, as all the previous times? Was this a vision, or is this reality? What was she trying to convey? Where was she taking her?" Carolina was not a runner and this excursion on foot was excruciating. She ran as far as she could, but the pain of gasping for air mixed with the burning sensation in her calves and thighs finally got the best of her and she stopped. Carolina was now oblivious to her physical location. During her long distance run of several blocks, she did not pay attention to the landmarks or even the direction. But now, that was the least of her concerns. She was in survival mode, bent over clutching her pants and gasping for air.

When she was finally able, she stood and looked around. The cyclist had led her right back to Iglesia-de-Francisco, (the church of San Francisco.) A few meters from the door was a bike rack, with one lone bike. Carolina instantly shrugged off the fatigue and sprung to life, heading directly toward the large wood door. Two police officers stood at the entrance smoking cigarettes. When Carolina arrived, they stepped in front of her blocking her access.

"You'll have to come back, the cathedral is closed." One of the officers gestured her to leave.

"Closed? You cannot close the house of God!" Carolina walked to within inches of the officer doing the speaking and looked him in the eye. "Under what authority?"

He didn't know what to say, or how to respond. His fingers went limp, releasing his smoldering cigarette which then fell to the bricks. His eyes grew wide and his pupils expanded. He turned to the other officer and spoke a couple of sentences, and then looked back at Carolina. "Please accept my apologies Senorita, you may enter." He reached out and grabbed the latch handle and opened the door, allowing Carolina to enter.

Carolina didn't know what came over her, nor did she take time to analyze the officer's sudden change of heart, she just kept walking down the large tapestry-lined corridor toward the large chapel. Carolina surmised because of similar physical features and dress, that the lone women that she saw the other day in the pew and the cyclist were indeed one and the same. And, she was hoping to confirm that speculation. But when she entered that grand room again, there was no woman present.

Carolina stood at the entrance to the gothic chapel and spanned the space, studying the pews of a virtually empty room, at least vacant of any female presence other than herself. There was a man lighting candles down front at the altar.

"This church is huge and with multiple chapels. Perhaps the cyclist was in another," Carolina thought she was about to turn around, but hesitated. As the other day, she felt something inviting about this room that enticed her to continue forward. Perhaps it was the sheer beauty of the architecture, the stained glass windows, or maybe it was as simple as yearning for her time spent in chapel at Notre Dame. Whatever it was she felt in harmony. Carolina walked all the way down front and sat in the second row of pews, directly behind the man who was now kneeling at the rail. Feeling at peace Carolina began meditating and praying, until her attention was altered as the man stood up. He straightened his trousers then inadvertently glanced in her direction. He acted a little surprised to see that he had company and reacted with a timid smile. He then approached and sat in the row directly in front of her. She tapped him on the shoulder and whispered, "I'm very sorry to startle you; I hope that you don't mind sharing this wonderful cathedral."

The man turned around and she immediately recognized his face. It was Luis Vargas! But it was his reaction that startled her. He instantly stood up, his eyes expanded wide and his face turned pale.

"Como hacer encontra mi?" There was a moment of awkward silence as they both stared at each other in astonishment. Luis nervously signed the cross across his chest, cleared his throat and then dropped to his knees. "How did you find me, Rebecca?" Carolina stepped back confused, while Luis squinted his eyes as if he were trying to adjust his focus.

"You are not Rebecca!" Noticeably embarrassed, Luis bowed his head, but then recoiled. "You are the journalist from Denver!" He stood up.

"How did you know where to find me? Who told you I was here? You must go, now!" Luis's demeanor changed from surprised to irritated, rattling off a salvo of questions and a demand.

"Please, Mr. Mayor, I had no idea that you were here." I am so sorry. I do want to interview you, but I would never invade your privacy or wish to deceive your trust to get an interview." Carolina paused. "You called me Rebecca. That's funny. Seems lately I remind everyone of a Rebecca, even back in Denver."

Luis shook his head and muttered, "Denver." "Who has put you up to this? Did Arthur send you? I told him I have no more money."

"I was sent by the *Denver Post* to interview you about the similarities of our cities as well as your personal relationship with Denver. I understand that you stayed with a family and attended high school there."

"Why did you not heed the warnings and immediately return to your country?" Luis reached out and grabbed the shoulders of Carolina. "I cannot bear the torture of another young life being lost."

Carolina pulled back and Luis's hands released their grip and his arms fell limp to his side.

"Heed what warnings, Sir?" Carolina looked at Luis puzzled.

"The message I… I mean, I was told was left on your mirror." Luis appeared nervous and uncomfortable.

"It was you who broke into my room and stole my belongings." Carolina was outraged.

"I had your belongings confiscated, only to protect you and frighten you into returning home. Bogotá is very unsafe. Drug Cartels, kidnappings and especially for those who choose to investigate my past. Your newspaper was not supposed to send a young woman! I specifically sent my letter to Editor Whitten."

"Well, if you wanted me to leave your county at once, why did you take my passport?" Carolina asked.

"Senorita, some mistakes were made, but I specifically instructed immigration to assist your embassy on obtaining you an immediate passport, which I understand is waiting for you."

"Why do you feel that I am in danger if I choose to investigate your past?" Carolina asked.

"There are those who profit from the security of secrets. Certainly your Mayor is one of them!"

Before Carolina had time to digest what Luis had just said, a loud bang rang out from behind them, causing both to look up. The source of the thunderous disturbance was Diego crashing though the large wood door, screaming in Spanish.

"I am very sorry, Mayor Vargas! This should have never happened! I had no idea how she was able to find you!" An excited Diego in full panic mode sprinted down the aisle toward them, followed closely by the two guards Carolina met at the door.

"Arrest her!" Diego ordered and the guards responded, reaching out, grabbing Carolina by the arm and pulling her from the pew.

"Stop! She poses no threat and this is the house of the Lord. All are welcome!" Vargas declared. The guards quickly unhanded her. "Release her, her arrest in most unnecessary." Luis Vargas commanded.

"But Mayor, she was clearly ..."

"Enough, Diego! Senorita, you must leave." Luis pointed toward the exit, and then turned his back.

"Yes Sir! Before I go may I get a picture of you? And once again I apologize." Vargas turned around, and she snapped a quick picture, then quickly put the camera in her bag.

"Carolina!" Diego reached his hand out and nodded, she took his direction, but not his hand. They walked side-by-side as he escorted her from the church and into the brick courtyard.

No words were spoken until they were outside, then Carolina unloaded, "So is that how friends treat friends here in Bogotá, Diego? Was it really necessary to suggest that I should be arrested? I had no idea that Vargas was in that church. It was merely coincidence we were both there at the same time. The nerve! Arrest me! I should have summoned the police to arrest him for authorizing a break-in of my hotel room and stealing my stuff! I probably should have had you arrested too! I'm sure that you were involved."

Carolina was clearly angered, but took a deep breath and gathered her emotions and regained her professionalism.

"How absurd! Mayor Vargas had nothing to do with the disappearance of your personal items! You misunderstood him! Because you have no witnesses to what you thought you heard, I suggest you never repeat that! My driver will take you to the American Embassy. You will pick up your temporary passport, then he will drive you to your hotel. You'll collect your bags. Then he will deliver you to the airport."

"So, I'm being deported for running into your Mayor in church?"

"No, we are merely assisting you in leaving our country because your visit is complete. Adios Senorita, Carolina!"

"Adios for now, Senor Diego!" Carolina marched off to the awaiting car.

CHAPTER 15

Carolina sent Whitten a quick email from the airport informing him that she was on her way home. And within a few hours from her unexpected encounter with Francisco Vargas she boarded a plane bound for the States.

After Carolina switched her phone to airplane mode she began jotting notes on a legal pad and had filled up six pages before the first beverage cart came around. She started with the ruse at Buenaventura and Captain Herrera Vargas's spontaneous inquiry 'asking if 'Arthur Higgins had sent her'. Next she questioned Diego's awareness of Denver's Homeless Coalition and drug cartels and she ended with Vargas's mysterious quote which she circled twice: "There are those who profit from the security of secrets. Certainly your mayor is one of them." After a break of mindless staring at nothing through the window, she started another page of descriptions and events.

Ignoring Diego, or Mayor Vargas, she concentrated on her cyclist friend. It included her dreams, her visions, and her encounters. The dates and times were all jotted alongside each particular occurrence. But there was one event that prompted her to garner a note to self, 'Find and read!' and she circled twice. It was the mysterious article which popped up on her screen back in her office, '***Young Denver woman goes into the record books, completing 7300-mile Cross-Country bicycle Journey***'.

Back in the States and specifically back in Denver, besides her family, no one was happier to see her than Karl Kaleido. Within seconds of the cab pulling up, he was on the sidewalk with open arms.

"The clouds have parted and my sunshine is back!" Karl gave Carolina a bear hug then grabbed her bags delivered to the curb by the cabby.

"Hi Karl, I missed you too! I appreciate it, but you do not need to get my luggage." Carolina patted him on the shoulder.

"My pleasure, Missy! Besides, you'll need both your hands to carry all your mail that I stowed away while you were gone. There's even a large package which arrived yesterday from Bogotá. I assume that you shipped something home so you wouldn't have to lug it through the airport."

Carolina shook her head. "I didn't sh..." Before she could finish her sentence, Karl opened the front door to the store and yelled at one of his employees.

"Fetch me sweet Carolina's mail box!"

Within seconds a more than eager young man came through the door carrying a large cardboard box filled with an assortment of envelopes and one large shipping box, which he secured by applying pressure with his chin. Karl motioned him to trek up the stairs and they both followed Carolina up to her door. When they arrived at the landing, Karl quickly set the bags down and stepped in front of Carolina.

"I guess that you know while you were gone your apartment was broken into. It was late at night I was coming back from a walk, looked up at your place and I saw flashlights, so I called the cops. I should have gone up there myself. By the time they arrived the thief was gone. Things are a mess inside, but the good thing is, your television and stereo are still there. So maybe they got scared away before they had a chance to take anything. By-the-way, once you do your initial inspection you are supposed to call this officer so he can complete his paperwork." Karl reached into his pocket and pulled out a card and a set of keys. He turned around and unlocked the door, then handed her the keys along with the police officer's card.

Carolina slowly entered the room. She was filled with feelings of déjà vu. Karl followed her in, placing the two pieces of luggage on the bed and the box of mail was subsequently placed in a chair by his subordinate. She took a few seconds to scan the room, and then began picking up papers and clothes which were tossed everywhere. Karl was right. None of her electronics were missing, actually nothing was missing, but her personal belongings had all been ransacked. This made her very uneasy, probably more so, than if her TV or her stereo had been stolen. Whoever had done this wasn't after valuable merchandise, they were after her personal information.

"Can we help you clean up?" Asked Karl

"Thanks guys! But, I think that this is a one person job. You are so sweet!"

"No need to thank us," Karl winked. "We will now get out of your hair and let you clean-up the mess and unpack. If you are not too tired later, the boys and I will be firing up the barbeque grill after we close shop. We'd love your company."

"I just may join you," Carolina smiled.

"Great! I can't wait to hear about your adventure or at least a preview of the highlights before I read about it in the paper." Karl excused himself and the two men exited her apartment.

Carolina closed the door behind her guests then immediately spun around and made a beeline toward the chair. She picked up the FedEx package, then walked over and set on her bed. She inspected the package briefly, and then tore open the end. Folded securely in bubble wrap were very familiar contents. It was her personal belongings that were stolen from her hotel room.

Carolina immediately turned the box upside down and shook it until confirmed that she had inventoried all of the contents. Beside her lay her jump drives, voice recorder, passport and even an envelope of her cash, to the exact dollar. Something else accompanied her personal items. It was a sealed envelope, hand written in English and addressed specifically to her, Carolina Paige. Carolina cautiously picked it up and with the nail of her index finger she carefully slit open and separated the sealed surfaces. She wanted to avoid needlessly tearing the envelope or the contents, because she had no idea what she'd find and what would require further scrutiny. Once she opened the flap, she pulled out the stationery and immediately recognized it.

It appeared to be similar parchment and perhaps the same hand writing as the letter she had examined which was sent to the *Post*, specifically to Whitten. One difference she didn't remember seeing from the first letter was the hieroglyphic like embroidery around the borders. She smoothed out the folds and began reading.

"My dear Senorita Paige, I want to apologize for the grotesque way that you were treated in my city, admittedly mostly due to my unacceptable behavior. My personal circumstances are no excuse for the way I've allowed a guest in my city to be treated. The guilt that I've been bearing for years has taken a toll on me and I am at my wits end. My rational thought process has all but left me. For years I've been living a lie, paying for a debt of my past, all to protect my fortune and the honor of my family name. I've allowed Arthur Higgins to control my life, my soul. Circumstances have now changed and it's not about the money anymore. Even maintaining my family's honor has less importance. I've been praying for years, for God to forgive me and I believe that he has. I have also been praying for courage to put an end to this farce, to free me from my debt on earth and finally he has. I find it amusing, the irony he's challenged me with, however."

"You see, finding out that I'm dying has given me an abundance of courage to set the record straight. I think the phrase you Americans like to use is 'turn the tables.' Perhaps it's revenge, but I prefer to think of it as an opportunity to tell my side of the story and finally expose any and all secrets. You have no idea how many years I have waited to purge this heavy burden from my soul.

"My original plan was to expose him, to humiliate him publically, and to end the years of great pain, extortion and blackmail. My intention was to invite Martin Whitten from the *Post* here, so that I could confess to the newspaper of the town in which Higgins is mayor, the town where this hideous event all started. I felt it was most important to give some sort of closure to the family of Rebecca. I wanted to show the people of Denver, Colorado just what kind of horrible hombre he really is. But, my plan never included endangering another innocent life in the process. My people were telling me that the *Post* was sending a journalist to write disparaging lies and propaganda, connecting me with FARC, the Revolutionary Armed Forces of Colombia. They wanted to 'deal with you,' the journalist. I knew that I couldn't stop them. When the *Post* sent you, a young senorita and not Martin Whitten, well the guilt came pouring in and

I felt a strong conviction to change my plan! Then during our chance encounter at Iglesia-de-Francisco, I actually had a vision, I thought you were her. I knew immediately God was sending me a message that I was doing the right thing. I had to get you out of my country and fast."

"By the time you will have received this package, I will have left this world. For years I have lost control of my life, so for my grand exit, I have decided that the last thing I do, I would be in control. Thus I have prepared to depart earlier than what the doctors had predicted. I know God will take issue, but I'm prepared to debate that subject with Saint Peter."

"I want you to expose everything you can about your corrupt Mayor, so that he will receive the proper humiliation and punishment that he deserves!"

"I have two more requests, I want the good people of Denver to know that I was not driving the car. Finally, please see that all which is in this account be given to the family of Ms. Wilson, just a meager gesture for their suffering."

Sincerely,

Luis Francisco Vargas

CHAPTER 16

Carolina's phone rang for several seconds before she snapped out of her deep train of thought after absorbing what she had just read.

"Hello."

"Paige?"

"Yes, Mr. Whitten, I just got home and I have so much…"

Whitten interrupted her before she could finish her sentence. "Mayor Luis Vargas is dead!"

"Yes I know," Carolina softly replied.

"How did you find out? I just received an email from the investigators I hired and they said the Bogotá press doesn't even know yet."

"Luis Vargas told me! I just read his letter."

"Don't go anywhere. I am on my way over!" Whitten abruptly ended the call, and Carolina set the phone beside

Scott Baker Sweeney

her on the bed. As she did, she noticed the camera that was also lying there and realized that she had not yet viewed the photos she snapped, including the one of Vargas in the church. But as she started to pick up the camera, a notion occurred to her.

"DIEGO!" She voiced out loud, and then thought to herself. "I've got to call Diego." She picked up her phone and dialed his number from her contact list, but it went directly into his voicemail.

"Diego, it's Carolina, I just heard the horrific news and I'm in shock. My deepest condolences. Please call me when you have a chance." Carolina proceeded to clean up the mess in her apartment while waiting on Whitten. Thirty minutes later she heard her door bell.

"Hi Boss."

"I'm glad you're back, Paige! Back safe, that is! So, your first real assignment turned out to be very exciting, right?"

"And, it's far from over." Thanks for trusting me with this and allowing me to go." Carolina offered him a seat in the only chair in her apartment, and then she sat on the corner of the bed.

"Well, I gotta tell you one more time that sending you off to Colombia by yourself was one of the dumbest

108

things that I've ever done. It should have never happened. But, what's done is done."

Carolina opened her laptop with one hand and held her legal pad in the other. She proceeded to review every detail of her trip from concise notes, regardless that she had already shared most of it in their earlier email or phone conversations. Whitten periodically stopped her and asked her to elaborate, or solicit her opinion. When she was done with her notes, she handed him the letter from Vargas which he carefully read. While he read the letter, she leafed to the second page of her legal pad revealing the sketches and notes of her reoccurring encounters with the female cyclist. She continued to omit these encounters from her summary.

"Do you have something more?" Whitten inquired. Carolina was startled. She didn't realize he was through reading Vargas's letter and was now staring at her gazing at the yellow notepad.

"Uh, yes sir, that's it! Oh wait!" Carolina ran into her kitchenette and grabbed a plastic bag and then returned to her makeshift desk/bed, where she carefully picked up the envelope and handed both items to Whitten. "Here's the envelope belonging to the letter and a bag to keep them from getting more contaminated with fingerprints.

I assume that you will probably want to have an expert compare both this letter to the other Bogotá letter. Your hired Colombian private investigators will be able to confirm hand writing and perhaps any finger prints left behind."

Whitten smiled, "Indeed, safety aside, I did select the right journalist to send to Bogotá after all. Paige, I'm impressed!"

"Because of Mayor Vargas's suicide I guess that I will be going back sooner than I thought. I'll make the arrangements first thing in the morning, Boss."

"Not so fast Paige! Now it's time for me to tell you about the rest of my phone call with the Colombian investigators. Seems the 'good Mayor's' advisors and staff, specifically your friend Diego Morales are blaming a female FARC sympathizer masquerading as a journalist from the *Denver Post* for his death. They will soon be issuing a warrant for her arrest once the news is released to the media."

Carolina jumped up. "What? My arrest? BASED ON WHAT EVIDENCE?! We must immediately send them this letter from Vargas to clear my name!" She began pacing the floor. "By the way, I just left a message on

Diego's cell phone." Whitten quickly responded with an assertive voice.

"We will, when the time is appropriate. We need to see what the official charges are first, so we know precisely the best and most appropriate manner in which to proceed. When we have obtained all of the evidence, I will discuss this with my superiors at the *Post* as well as our legal team on how to proceed."

"I was hoping that you had not tried to contact Diego yet. Paige, there is a strong chance that Colombian officials, or maybe worse, the cartels will offer a bounty for your return. If that's the case, we will need to move you underground. They most likely have technology to track your phone, so no more answering incoming or making outgoing calls. Last week after the break-ins and death threats, I notified the private protection firm used often by the *Post* to watch our places at night. I've stepped that up today to also guard you."

"So will he be sleeping in a chair outside my door too?" Carolina smirked.

"What's that, Paige?"

"Nothing, Boss. I look forward to meeting him."

Whitten looked from side-to-side at the mess, and said. "You need to call the police officer assigned to your case as soon as you can, but don't use your phone."

"Yes, Sir. Boss, Vargas's letter mentioned FARC and now you tell me Diego accuses me of being a FARC spy or sympathizer of sorts. I don't believe it's a coincidence. It sounds like an important lead. I guess I need to step up my research on the 'Revolutionary Armed Forces of Colombia'."

"So back to your conversation with the Colombian PI's, did Vargas leave a note at the scene? Also, how did he commit the act?" Carolina asked.

"They were unsure on the note, but the unofficial report was a bullet to the head." Whitten answered.

Carolina paused for a minute to reflect, and then continued. "Boss, his letter to me said that he was terminally ill. We need to find out what disease? It should be easy to locate his personal doctor. Colombian Physicians aren't committed to governmental privacy laws like we are here in the States."

"Noted. Actually, I will forward you my contact information and you can take over the communication with them. I'll tell them to expect your call. After you make your call to the police *on a land line*, get down to the *Post* and stop by I.T.! Exchange your phone for a secure one. Oh yes, Carolina, what about pictures?"

"I haven't had time to look at my photos yet" Carolina responded as she reached for her camera, but then her phone rang.

"Don't answer," Whitten ordered.

"I know," Carolina picked up the phone to look at the incoming number. "It's Diego!" They both stared at the device until it stopped buzzing. Then they waited, staring longer waiting for a voicemail alert which never came.

"Return his call from a secure landline at the *Post*. In fact we'll set up a line so we can record your conversation." Whitten stood up and started to leave.

"Don't you want to see the pictures?" Carolina held up the camera and Whitten hesitated, but then proceeded to his exit.

"Print them and leave a copy on my desk."

Carolina also stood up and looked around the room, then thought to herself, "This mess can wait! I guess I'll go use Karl's landline to check with the investigating cop and perhaps grab a hamburger before I head to the *Post*."

CHAPTER 17

S he opened the door and started down the steps to see the guys at Kaleidospokes, but to her surprise a very large burley individual was waiting for her at the bottom. She froze! He was dressed in jeans and a white tee-shirt covered by a lofty blue sports coat which could double as a circus tent.

"I'm Bruce Watt with Mile High Security." The man reached in his jacket and pulled out a badge and a card.

"I'll leave this on the step and back away several feet so that you can come down and read my credentials."

"You stay put, Carolina!" From the side of the building walked Karl and three of his mechanics. Each individually armed with their own choice of weaponry, Karl with a Louisville Slugger and the other three guys had a fire extinguisher and two bicycle chains. The large man recoiled and slipped his hand back under his jacket.

"Stop!" Carolina cried out. "Just everyone, stop!" She resumed walking down the steps and picked up the credentials.

"Karl, Guys, it's okay! The *Post* sent this gentleman to watch the apartment and me as a precaution after what happened. He's from a reputable security firm."

The large man chimed in, "You are welcome to call the number on my photo I.D. card to verify who I am."

"That won't be necessary Mr. Watt. I was expecting you. You just gave me a start," Carolina responded.

"Actually, it looks like you don't need my services." The large man looked at Carolina and smiled. Then he looked back at the gang from Kaleidospokes.

"Well, I guess we haven't done such a great job, letting her place get robbed and ransacked. So, welcome aboard Mr. Watt. Now that we are one big happy family, let's go eat some burgers." Karl said as he and his three amigos lowered their improvised weapons and marched away.

"Shall we?" Carolina brushed shoulders with Big Bruce as she walked past him. He in turn followed and they caught up with the gang.

Karl put the closed sign in the door and within minutes the grill out back was hot, the beer was cold and the music was loud. "Opa!" Karl exclaimed and with that, Carolina forgot about making her phone calls.

CHAPTER 18

"So Missy, tell me about your trip to Colombia," Karl asked handing Carolina a glass of wine.

"Thank you, Karl. Well, it was quick, but exciting. You would have loved it. There were people on bicycles everywhere. I even got to fly over the Andes in a small plane. I must say, that was a little frightening."

"Yes, Colombia, that was a trip that was never made." With that statement Karl seemed to fade away in a daydream, gazing off into space. Sensing he had drifted away, Carolina reached out and grabbed his hand.

"Are you okay, Karl? I've seen that far away look from you before. I think it was the last time I mentioned bicycles in Colombia."

"Yes, I'm sorry Carolina; it just brings back old memories that send my mind into trance. You see, way back in another lifetime, I too was planning a trip to

Bogotá to rendezvous with a very close friend. Actually, she was my fiancée… Rebecca, my sweet Becky. We planned to be wed there. She had just completed a consecutive tour from coast-to-coast across the United States. She pedaled more than 7300 miles in one hundred and nine days, and was training to be the first to cycle from the farthest point in North America to the farthest point in South America." Karl took a deep breath and hesitated before continuing, "Then, she was taken from me! The bicycle hanging from the ceiling belonged to Rebecca."

"Rebecca…Becky!" Carolina gasped! Her intuition anticipated his admission but nevertheless when he mentioned the name Rebecca it iced her to the bones. She recalled reading a brief newspaper article recognizing this event that appeared out of nowhere on her computer screen. At the time she didn't realize the significance.

Karl's eyes widened when she blurted out Rebecca's name. "Excuse me?" Karl looked at her bewildered.

"Sorry, Karl, you reminded me of something I read while researching my article." Embarrassed by her outburst, she nervously replied, I'm sorry Karl. I wish that I could stay longer. I really want to talk more about this later, but I must get to the office. Thank you for the glass of Chianti. I'll just grab Big Bruce and we'll be on our way."

One benefit to having a full time bodyguard which Carolina was now recognizing was that she was also getting a chauffeur too. Carolina climbed into the passenger side of Bruce's sedan, with her backpack, laptop and camera and they headed to the *Post*.

"Actually Bruce, I could get used to being driven around like this. This is great! It's a lot better than a cab and owning a car is way overrated!" They both laughed. Carolina reached in her backpack and pulled out her camera.

"Finally a chance to browse my pictures," Carolina muttered then she began scrolling from frame to frame and for a block or two the car was very quiet.

"Oh my God, it's Rebecca!" Carolina's voice was sharp and quivered as she startled Bruce with her sudden exclamation.

"What's wrong Miss?"

"Nothing Bruce, I'm sorry. I am a little surprised that I picked up something on this one shot, that I didn't realize that I had captured."

"Well I hope that's a good thing, Miss. Regardless, we're about a block away."

Bruce took one of the reserved spaces in the parking garage and they both hoofed it to the elevators, then on to her office. It was late and many of the eight-to-fivers were gone. Carolina went into her office and Bruce took a seat outside of her door. After she straightened the clutter on her desk and quickly shuffled through her mail. She was on to the first thing on her to-do list, and that was research. "What is FARC?" Carolina typed that question into the *Post's* search engine. Immediately an abundance of information was in front of her, including the answer to her question.

'FARC is the acronym for Revolutionary Armed Forces of Colombia, or the Spanish pronunciation, Fuerzas Armadas Revolucionarias de Colombia.' Carolina scanned through everything she could find about this organization. When she saw something of importance, she copied and pasted it on a word document that she would save in her notes.

"The guerilla organization came into existence around 1964. They claim to be an army of peasant Marxists with a radical political platform. They were very aggressive and imposed their will with violence. They have been known to employ a variety of military tactics, most deemed unconventional including terrorism. Their main source of funding came from kidnapping for ransom, extortion and the distribution of illegal drugs, making them the most dangerous of the Colombian cartels. They have a long history of violence, hideous crimes, drug wars and attempted civil wars."

One of the most interesting things she found and highlighted was supposedly in 2012 there was a truce announced between FARC and the Colombian Government. FARC would no longer participate in kidnappings of military personnel or police officers. The one thing that wasn't covered in the truce was discontinuing their other criminal activities against private civilians which included hundreds of hostages still being ransomed. Those crimes continued.

Carolina plugged her camera into the computer then sent the photos to the printer. She wanted to have them on Whitten's desk when he arrived first thing in the morning. Carolina reached inside her purse and pulled out the investigating police officer's card.

"I need to get this over with." Carolina thought remembering Whitten's orders. She picked up the rarely used, *Denver Post* line phone sitting on the corner of her desk and called the officer in charge of her apartment burglary. His questions took a total of about thirty seconds and his lack of enthusiasm made her realize that this crime would most likely be filed in the, unsolved category.

Carolina suddenly realized another call she needed to make, a call home to her parents. She stood and walked over to close her door for this private conversation. Of course she had no plans of disclosing any of the ominous events that happened. She felt that would come after this entire event was history. She knew that worrying them would serve no benefit to either parent or child. Their phone conversation lasted for almost ninety minutes and covered every topic under the sun. Even though nothing of significant substance was covered, it comforted her tremendously.

After speaking with her parents, Carolina was ready to summon Bruce and head for home. In her haste she forgot to pull the photos off the printer.

"Okay Bruce, are you ready to drive me home?" She opened her door to find her bodyguard half asleep in the chair with a copy of yesterday's paper in disarray, all over his chest, beside him and on the floor below. Bruce jumped up startled, sending the papers flailing. After the blood returned to his brain and he realized there was no imminent danger, his face turned scarlet with embarrassment.

Bruce drove Carolina home, parking his car out front on the curb. They inconspicuously walked past the Kaledeispokes soiree, still in full force, up the steps and to her door. Bruce made Carolina wait outside on the landing while he inspected her apartment. He soon returned, let her in, wished her a goodnight, then assumed his overnight position in his car, but not before setting up a temporary sensor on her door which would send an alarm signal to his phone.

CHAPTER 19

The night went quickly and was uneventful, even in Carolina's dreams. She was exhausted and appreciated not having any interruptions from her new friend. She even lightheartedly whispered toward the wall, "Thank you, Rebecca."

Big Bruce on the other hand, didn't see many sheep that night. He drove Carolina to work, escorted her to her office, then left, but not before issuing her orders.

"You're safe here. I need to go home, shower and get a few hours of sleep. I'll be back this afternoon to take you home. Unless the building is on fire, do not leave! Do not use the restroom without taking someone with you. DO NOT GO ANYWHERE IN THIS BUILDING ALONE!"

"Affirmative, Captain!" She saluted.

As she watched him walk to the elevator she began formulating a list in her mind of all the things she needed to accomplish that day. At the top of that list was collecting the Colombia photographs she left in the printer and delivering them to Whitten. She navigated her way through the maze of cubicles, greeting her coworkers as she went finally arriving at her destination, the copy room. Waiting for her on one of the photo printers were her pictures. Grabbing the photos and forgetting everything that Bruce had instructed, she went to the elevators, solo, to take her short trip to Whitten's floor. While on the elevator she sorted through the photos until she came to the one of Vargas in the church.

Carolina was so engrossed examining the photo that the elevator door opened at Whitten's floor, then closed without her even noticing. The image of Rebecca in the picture of Vargas was no longer there. After a quick trip to the top floor and back she finally exited on Whitten's floor. Deep in revelation she nearly walked past his office too. "Perhaps the image still exists on my camera," she thought.

"You look far away, Paige." Whitten growled from behind his desk.

"I'm sorry Sir, just a thousand things on my mind."

"No worries, just my observation. Whatcha got for me?"

"Here are the photos from the trip, including a candid shot of Luis Vargas. Photography is not my strong suit, however I think there's a couple of shots we can use." Whitten grabbed the photos from Carolina and took his turn at reviewing.

"So I understand you've met Bruce. Is everything kosher with him?"

"Bruce is BIG," Carolina smiled.

"Good! So what's on your agenda today?"

"Well, after I exchange my phone, I plan to visit my friends at the Homeless Coalition. I also plan to call Mayor Higgins office to set up an interview with the honorable one, or at the very least, get a statement on Vargas death. Do you think you could copy me that old Polaroid of the two boys you received from Bogotá? And Sir, as soon as possible, I want to call Diego. Do you want to set up a special *Post* landline? Special as in recorded?"

"Yes, I'll make arrangements to set up a line. As far as a copy of the Polaroid, done! Got it in an envelope already. And the call to Diego, our policy and the law is we need to ask permission from the person on the other end, in this case Diego to record the conversation. So, in case you may not get his permission, I'll listen in. Our policies are a little grayer when it comes to a third party who happens to be in the room and catches a conversation on a speaker phone." Whitten winked.

Carolina exchanged her phone, then grabbed her gear and once again deliberately disobeyed Bruce by calling for a cab. Her destination was Homeless Coalition office in the City County Building.

"Hey I know you," excitedly opined the silver-haired gentleman from behind the desk.

"Well hello, James," smiled Carolina.

"I bet you're here to see the Mrs."

"You bet correctly. Is she in?"

"Of course. You can head on up." Instead of Carolina walking toward the elevators, she walked closer to Jame's desk.

"Tell me James, how often does Mayor Higgins stop by the Homeless Coalition office?"

Because of the open atrium, James could look up and see just about every office door on every floor.

"Well, the funny thing is, he normally only goes in there right before he heads out on his fishing trip. However, today was one of those rare occasions, because he just got back from his trip and he had already been there two weeks ago. Today he was there for quite some time. In fact, he just left. Kind of a crazed look on his face too, I mean more than his normal crazed look," James chucked.

"Anything you want me to pass on to your better half today, James?"

"Tell her to throw me down a sandwich."

Carolina laughed and nodded, already walking to the elevators. "Thanks for the tidbit on our Mayor."

Carolina stepped off the elevator at the same time as Elizabeth was locking the glass door of the Coalition office. As she pulled her keys out of the lock, she turned and was surprised to see Carolina standing there with a warm smile.

"Well, if it isn't the bad-timing reporter from the *Post!*" Elizabeth said disgustingly.

"I am very sorry for stopping by unannounced. I just have a few questions. Do you mind if I walk with you?"

"That's fine dear and I am sorry too. I didn't mean to be so rude. It's that, there are so many things going on. Bad day! Bad week! And, I am sick of all the shit around here! Actually, you stopping by is great timing." Elizabeth stepped around Carolina, her eyes welled with tears. She grabbed Carolina's arm and gently pulled her along into the elevator. "Hell yes, you can tag along, get out your notepad, I've got a lot to say." Elizabeth completely broke down on the elevator and when the door opened on the lower floor James witnessed her exit with Carolina consoling her. He immediately jumped up and rushed to her side.

"Sweetheart, what's wrong?" James bent over to look into the eyes of his wife, and then he looked at Carolina, who responded by shaking her head.

"I'm okay darling," Elizabeth said softly. "I just lost it." Carolina handed her a tissue and they walked over to sit on a close bench.

"This has got something to do with that arrogant, S.O.B. Mayor doesn't it? I should march right up there to his office and give him a little of his comeuppance," James stated.

"It's okay James. I'm okay! I'll explain tonight. Go back to your desk. Ms. Paige and I need to talk." Elizabeth patted her husband on the back. "I'm okay you big lug, now get back to work!" Elizabeth smiled, assuring her husband that everything was fine. He reluctantly walked back to his desk.

"There's a café across the street. How about a cup of coffee?" Carolina asked.

"Coffee sounds good!"

CHAPTER 20

Mid-morning was good for getting an immediate table. They were ahead of the lunch crowd, the café was quiet and most importantly, there was no one there whom she knew from the City and County Building. They were seated in a booth near the back of the restaurant. They both ordered their coffee and a slice of pie. Moments of silence went by as neither women spoke. Carolina could tell that Elizabeth was piecing together what she was going to say and she didn't want to pressure her.

Finally after a few moments of staring into her coffee, Elizabeth spoke. "You know, I've worked for this damn city and that damn Mayor for over twenty years. I've been a loyal and dedicated employee for The Denver Homeless Coalition for the last twelve. I've looked the other way on, let's just say, less than scrupulous activities, but that all ends today! There were large amounts of cash coming in and large amounts of cash going out. Whenever I asked Higgins for receipts, I would get chastised. Because the Homeless Coalition is independently funded, nonprofit, guidelines are a whole lot less scrutinized than any other agency across the street. Hell, our year end auditing is not prepared by the city auditors. It's done mostly by the mayor. I do see it though, and most of the cash transactions are never reported. I should say that one ominous and continuous cash debit is never reported."

"Where is that cash going?" Carolina interrupted.

"It's more like, where was the cash going to? When Higgins stopped by today, I assumed he was going to purge the safe of cash again. When I commented about seeing him so soon since his last withdrawal, he became belligerent, screaming at me and calling me an ignorant whore. He told me that for the record, there wouldn't be any need for additional large cash expenditures or withdrawals and he suggested that I would be wise never to bring that up again. Before he stormed out the door he had the nerve to threaten me by saying, 'by the way, there seems to be a great deal of cash missing from the safe' and that he would hate to turn me into the police, before terminating my employment. I've got news for him, I quit!"

"Did he say why there would not be any more need for large cash withdrawal? Did anyone else witness or hear him?" Carolina asked.

"No, he never said and I, well I really didn't give a damn at that point. I was the only one in the office. The two other gals are off today. I'll take a damn lie detector test!"

"How many other people know the combination to the safe?"

"Just Higgins and me. We are the only two."

"So again, where do you think the cash was going?"

Elizabeth paused and sat back while the waitress refilled her cup. "I think our glorious Mayor is buying large amounts of drugs from Colombia, either for his personal habit or to sell or both." Elizabeth's voice was trembling.

"How much cash is he lifting from the safe?" Carolina continued.

"It varies, but it's usually fifty to one hundred thousand around eight to ten times a year. But Ms. Paige, that is not all. A lot of our contributors including major businesses have set up automatic monthly withdrawals from credit cards. But what they didn't pay attention to is there's a secondary name on their account statement and only a portion of the funds remain in the Homeless account. The rest pass through and are transferred to another account."

"What's the name on that account?"

"Fuerzas Armadas!" Elizabeth hesitated then continued. "Way back when, I asked Higgins about this, he gave me some B.S. that the Armadas account was for training and relocating many of the homeless candidates to South America. How absurd, right? Relocating our poor and homeless with access to loads of government programs to a semi-third world country with no programs, makes a whole lot of sense. I guess that the climate would be a lot more conducive there for living under a bridge." It was obvious that Elizabeth's sarcastic tone was directed at herself. She hesitated deep in thought before continuing, "Of course there were never any receipts or data justifying this nonsense. Something else, I have a strong suspicion that all of the homeless applicants' personal information was compromised. This digital information was supposed to be stored securely, but a couple of times when I accessed it to add applicants' information, I found that others had previously been there, by the shading of data, showing that someone was copying it. Unless it was hacked, the only two people with the access password are Higgins and me."

"What about the others who serve on the commission board? Do they ever question any of this?" After Carolina asked this question, Elizabeth rolled her eyes and snickered.

"Are you kidding me? Other than a couple of local clergy, the board consists of 'yes' men and political see-nothing, hear-nothing and say-nothing suits. Let me clarify. This commission brings in ten to twelve million annually. They're not going to miss a couple two or three million, especially if Mayor Higgins is cooking the books."

"Why have you not said anything before now?"

Elisabeth went silent for a minute, staring impassively past Carolina and into oblivion, until her eyes misted over, then gravity streamed her tears down her cheeks. "Because I also helped myself to some of the cash," Elizabeth broke down, sobbing.

"One time is all, I swear! The bastard said I could, it would be my bonus, he said. I'm such an idiot! Of course now he claims that he never said anything and he kept the security camera video to hold over me."

"Elizabeth, listen to me. You need to hire a good attorney. If you want, the *Post* can help you with that. Will you give me permission to quote you and what you've just told me?" Carolina handed her a tissue.

"Yes, of course."

"Go home now. I'll tell James that you're okay. Here's my phone number, call me if you need anything. I was planning on calling the Mayor's office to ask him a few questions regarding his so called fishing trip to Colombia and to get his thoughts on the death of Bogotá's mayor, but instead, I think I'll just stop by. Don't worry, I won't ask him anything that you've disclosed to me."

CHAPTER 21

Carolina parted ways with Elizabeth and marched back across the street to the City and County building. She momentarily stopped to talk to James, and then jumped on the elevator to the top floor and the office of Mayor Higgins.

When she opened the door he was actually standing behind the receptionist's desk conversing with a staffer which created an awkward moment for both him and the receptionist. The receptionist immediately looked at him for consent before acknowledging Carolina. Higgins didn't respond.

"May I help you?"

"Yes you can. I'm Carolina Paige from the *Denver Post*." She handed the receptionist her card. "I apologize for just barging in. I happened to be in the building for other business and I thought I would take a chance of stopping by to see if I could catch the Mayor in his office and it looked like I lucked out." Carolina smiled and half-heartedly pointed in Higgins direction. Higgins carried on his conversation with the staffer un-phased by Carolina's introduction.

"Mayor Higgins normally doesn't take cold calls from the press. What is the order of your business?" Asked the receptionist in a deliberate tone.

Carolina leaned over and whispered, "I promise, I'm usually not this forward. Next time I will make sure to make an appointment." Then Carolina resumed her more assertive voice to answer the receptionist's question, raising her volume a notch to assure that the mayor would have no problem hearing. And he didn't. "I was wondering if the mayor would like to make a statement or reaction to the sudden death of his friend Mayor Vargas of Bogotá, Colombia." Higgins immediately stopped and looked in her direction.

"We were hardly friends." Higgins announced.

He immediately ended his conversation with the staffer and walked around the receptionist's desk, snatching up Carolina's card, then stepped directly in front of Carolina. He stood almost toe-to-toe with her staring at her card for a couple of seconds before looking at her.

I Was Never Afraid

"Ms. Paige, you are not the reporter who normally is assigned to me from the *Post*. The mayor took a step back, looking her over from head to toe, as if he were a judge inspecting a state fair calf.

"No Sir, I'm a journalist not a beat writer. I grant you, there's not a whole lot of difference, except I cover a variety of stories, not just one topic or subject." Carolina smiled, hoping to get a reaction from the Mayor, but she wasn't successful. He continued coldly staring into her eyes, so she resumed.

"I'm actually doing research to write two stories. One relates to the success of Denver's Homeless Coalition. I know, another article, right? How many articles can the *Post* write about this subject?" Carolina shook her head and smiled, still no reaction from Higgins. "Well then there's the second article. The funny thing is I actually stumbled upon this while I was collecting information on the first story. And this story is way more interesting than another article touting the successes of the Coalition. The thing is, the stories might even share relevance. Mr. Mayor, I found out about your relationship with Mayor Vargas of Bogotá Colombia. I found out that you've gone fishing with him on several occasions over the years and that you both share similar policies regarding care for

139

the homeless. You know this is like peeling an onion, the more I peel, the more layers I find."

Carolina's attempt to extract enough ire from the mayor to either move their discussion to his office or to get her escorted from his office was beginning to work. He broke his stare and was beginning to fidget, so she continued.

"I had planned on setting up an appointment to interview you and get your comments, but when the shocking news came over the wire about Bogotá's Mayor Vargas and I was already down here at the Homeless Coalition's office, well ..." That was it. He had heard enough. He cleared his throat and touched her shoulder to direct her toward his office.

"Yes, of course, let's continue this conversation in my office."

"But Sir, what about your two o'clock?" The receptionist, who couldn't help but overhear Carolina's spiel, interrupted the Mayor.

"It's okay Karen, my two o'clock can wait!" The Mayor snapped.

Mayor Higgins, extended his hand, indicating to Carolina to enter his large windowed office. Then he pointed to a posh leather chair positioned in front of his mahogany desk. As she proceeded to sIt down he closed the door and headed for his chair. The view was breathtaking of downtown Denver, but the ambiance didn't break her focus. Higgins rolled his chair up and placed his arms on the desk, then inhaled a deep breath followed by a slow exhale.

"So you came here looking for a quote, a statement that you can print in your paper exposing my deepest thoughts regarding the Good Mayor Luis Francisco Vargas's sudden demise. I'm sure that you are aware that your paper has done several articles over the years of my fishing expeditions to Colombia. They even stumbled into the fact that I've fished a few times with the mayor of Bogotá. That's nothing top secret. I've fished with several people over the years. Why do you presume that I had some special relationship?"

Carolina said nothing, reached into her purse and pulled out the digital copy of the Polaroid, stood up and plopped it down on the desk in front of him. Higgins glanced down, then back at Carolina. She picked the photo up and deposited it back into her purse.

"That was a long time ago and one might even say another life time ago. My parents opened up our home to Luis so that he could receive an American education.

For four years the young boys in the photo shared a home, a bedroom and a bathroom. We also shared a school, a neighborhood and even a car. But sometimes unexpected events dictate that things change. Sometimes, these events allow you to recognize someone for the real person he is. A betrayal of trust separated those two boys in that photo."

"Did you ever try to mend your relationship, perhaps during one of your fishing trip?"

Higgins sarcastically chucked. "Some betrayals can never be mended. You may not believe me, but there was never a real relationship after our childhood. That includes fishing trips. And, that's all I have to say about our personal relationship, none of which I wish to be printed in the paper. This is off the record and if you publish any of this, at best I'll never grant you another interview." The mayor continued. "If it's a quote for your article that you've come looking for, here it is, and when I conclude you may leave." He reflected a moment then cleared his throat and Carolina pulled out her recorder.

"'I am distressed to hear of the passing of Mayor Luis Francisco Vargas, of Bogotá Colombia. Our relationship over the years has been cordial and he will be missed. And for the record, I will not be attending his memorial." Carolina clicked off her recording device.

"Sir, are you sure that you don't want to elaborate on your childhood relationship? What caused the bitterness between you? Would you like to comment on your Homeless Coalition? I understand Mayor Vargas tried to create his own version in Bogotá. Did he seek your advice?" Carolina rattled off a quick barrage of questions, but was careful not to reveal Vargas' letter or what Elizabeth had divulged to her earlier. She wanted so bad to drop the name "Fuerzas Armadas" to see his reaction, but refrained. Higgins pushed the chair back from his desk, then stood up.

"Ms. Paige you have over-stayed your welcome and now I must ask you to leave." He thrust his arm out and pointed toward the door. She subsequently stood and smiled.

"Thank you very much for your time. But, if you change your mind and would like to share anything with the citizens of Denver the office, please don't hesitate, you have my card." Carolina stepped around the chair, opened the door, walked through the office, cordially gestured at the receptionist and marched to the elevator. Concerned about Elizabeth, and before exiting the building, Carolina walked to James station and instructed him to take care of his bride.

CHAPTER 22

O n the street side of the revolving door a surprise was waiting that she was not quite prepared for. As soon as she lifted her arm to hail a cab she felt two arms from behind slide simultaneously under each of hers, lifting her off of her heals. Two men, clinching her on each side, and briskly escorting her to an awaiting black limousine.

Despite being downtown Denver in the middle of the day and within a scream of a police officer or two, this happened so fast she did not have time to react.

The car door swung open and she was thrust into the dark galley. Carolina's head hit the console as the door slammed behind her. Immediately, the force of the car rapidly pulling away sent her pummeling to the floor. A hand reached down grabbing her wrist and pulled her up into the seat. Her hair was over her face restricting her sight, but that didn't stop her from lashing out in the direction of the arm, striking blows while voicing a litany of choice expletives. A moment later a cold steel cylinder pressed against her temple followed by a voice snarling out a sentence in Spanish. She had no idea what was said, but she had a pretty good idea what was implied and immediately ceased her retaliation.

"Perhaps you are now through with your tantrum and are now ready to be a good girl." Carolina recognized the English-speaking Colombian accent and slowly pulled her hair away from her eyes. As she did, a light came on revealing her guests as well as the familiar voice.

"Diego!" Carolina cringed.

The illuminated cabin revealed three dark complexioned men, two on each side of her and one facing her from the back of the limousine. The familiar voice spoke again and it came from a laptop computer held by the man sitting in the back. When Carolina turned her attention to the computer screen, she saw an arrogantly poised Diego Morales, via Skype.

"You know Senorita, it is terribly rude not to return one's call! However, I suppose that it is normal reaction after committing a crime."

"What are you saying and who are these men? Are they abducting me?" Carolina screamed.

"Senorita Paige, you are not just merely being abducted. We are arresting you for the murder of Mayor Francisco Vargas!" Diego chuckled. Diego nodded, prompting one of his thugs to pull out a pair of handcuffs. This action was countered by Carolina reaction. She jumped up and slid the patrician screen open and screamed, "Help me!" to the driver. But to no avail. Within seconds and a short struggle she was handcuffed.

Carolina screamed, "You cannot do this, I am a journalist for the *Denver Post*, and I have a body guard!" Diego and the three men erupted in laughter. In this circumstance, Carolina realized that her statement sounded ridiculous.

"I am innocent, surely you know that? The Associated Press announced that Vargas died of a self-inflicted gunshot to the head. He even left a note." Carolina continued. "You cannot take me from the United States against my will, I have rights! You'll never get me through Customs and on a plane."

"Senorita, patience. You soon will be privy to our plan. As far as your innocence, you have little evidence to support your claim. The Associated Press was wrong.

Anyone can write a note and pay someone to verify it. We have found conclusive evidence, such as your finger prints and your DNA at the crime scene." Carolina started to speak, but one of the men slapped her face and bound her mouth with duct tape.

"You have rudely interrupted me for the last time, so now you are done talking," Diego took a deep breath, before continuing. "My business venture has been disrupted resulting in two vital revenue streams ceasing. It's unfortunate, but I believe that the late mayor in his final letter has shared information that is detrimental to my existence; therefore I have only two options imprisoning you or killing you. Indeed your involvement with Mayor Vargas is regrettable. However I have figured a way to make your timely visit to Bogotá prove quite beneficial in the long run and allow my ventures to continue."

"Your immediate and trusted relationship with Mayor Vargas is quite unexplainable. Never-the-less it has occurred and now I must resolve it. And perhaps it may prove to be a much sounder arrangement than before. You had mentioned a note left by Senor Vargas at the time of his death, that note is inconsequential. The note that I am most interested in is the one that he sent you. Senor Vargas on his death bed revealed a self-described 'confessional letter' which he mailed to an 'entrusted confidant' in the U.S.A. I believe that ally is you, Senorita Paige. My associates checked your apartment for this letter, but did not find it. Are you in possession of this letter?"

One of the thugs grabbed her purse and began riffling through it, while Carolina wildly shook her head back and forth. He then dumped the contents on the seat beside him and began sorting through her belongings with his finger. He stopped briefly to view the Polaroid of the young boys, and then held it up in front of the screen so that Diego could view. Diego acknowledged but didn't comment.

"It's at your office, right?" Carolina said nothing. "The letter, it's at your office, correct?" The thug grabbed her by the back of the next and twisted. Carolina shrieked in pain, then nodded.

"Well, just a little wrinkle in my plan. Who needs a letter when you will tell the word what it says, when you are delivered to Bogotá. I pretty much know of its contents, anyway," Diego continued.

"You seem to be puzzled, as if you wish me to explain my intentions with you." Diego condescendingly toyed with Carolina. "You see it's all about finding a solution to the problem. Senor Vargas' early demise has presented me with problems. You Senorita are the useful solution. You will find out more, but all in good time."

"Oh yes, I feel that I must explain how I would transport you through customs and on to your new home in Colombia. You see, when you are presumed to be dead and in a casket, and there is no scent of narcotics it's really pretty simple." Carolina's eyes grew wide with fear.

"Oh fret not my young Senorita. Your demise is not imminent." Diego laughed. "My friends there will inject a serum that will slow your heart rate to be virtually undetectable. They'll plop you in a casket and then transport your corpse expediently through Customs, then onto our private jet." Carolina looked up to see one the thugs pulling out a syringe and she lost it. She took her leg and kicked the thug in the chin, sending the syringe flying. Then in one motion she was able to roll the corner of the tape away from her mouth with a rub on her shoulder and lunged toward the partition window, yelling again at the driver.

The commotion caused him to turn around taking his attention off the road. When he looked forward an obstacle appeared in the road which caused him to swerve and lose control. This abrupt action sent all of the occupants tumbling violently back and to the side just moments before the thugs could restrain her. She felt a jarring impact and the wild ride was over. All the occupants were deposited on the floor like ragdolls, including Carolina. Before they could react, she managed to pull herself up and back onto the seat and then slid over to the door where she grabbed the handle from behind with her cuffed hands and leaned back, hard.

Her momentum took her tumbling backward onto the street. She could hear a plethora of excited Colombian voices from inside the car, including the driver pleading in English that a bicycle pulled out in from of him causing this dilemma.

Carolina jumped up staggering backward with her arms behind her back and the piece of duct tape dangling from her mouth flapping in the breeze. With a quick survey of her situation she decided to sprint back across the busy divided highway. Traffic was her ally. The sound of screeching tires and honking horns filled the air within seconds. Vehicles were stopped all around her, giving her cover for her escape. Carolina weaved between the cars, and was nearly struck by a minivan. The driver rolled down her window to ask Carolina if she could assist but when the lady saw she was cuffed and with duct tape over half her mouth she roller her window back up and reached around to lock her door.

Carolina turned to look back to see if she was being pursued, but she wasn't, so she continued running parallel with the traffic. She could now hear sirens approaching and to her relief, she could see the flashing lights of a rescue vehicle barreling toward her down the shoulder.

Carolina was eventually approached by a couple of good Samaritans who removed the tape from her mouth and urged her to sit down on the asphalt and wait for the emergency vehicle to arrive.

For the moment Carolina's dramatic perils were over. Other than the red bump on her forehead from being forced in the car and the hand print across her cheek from the slap, she was unharmed.

She was immediately swarmed by EMT's, then moments later by Colorado State Police. Within moments of hearing her account, the police moved her to the safety of a police unit. They also closed the highway, changed the police description from an accident scene, to the scene of a kidnapping. Other crime units were notified including the FBI. They removed her handcuffs and took her report as well as assailant descriptions. She was there for what seemed to be an eternity.

The officer assigned to her allowed her to make a call on his cell phone to Whitten, so he could validate her identity and verify that she was an employee of the *Post*. The call prompted Whitten to get permission from the authorities to land their helicopter at the scene to pick up Carolina.

Within minutes after concluding the call, Whitten and Big Bruce arrived at the scene. After a brief identity verification with an officer guarding the car, Whitten climbed in the back with Carolina, while Bruce remained outside. Before any words were exchanged between Carolina and Whitten, a man in a suit approached the car, acknowledged the officer and Bruce then opened the passenger door and joined them.

He introduced himself as Inspector Miller of the Denver office of the FBI. He reached over the seat and handed Carolina her purse, cell phone and recorder. He then asked her to repeat the events which led to the limousine crashing into the concrete barrier wall.

Carolina told him that she would cooperate fully. And, she did just that. She explained everything which was pertinent, with the exception of her meeting with Elizabeth and Diego's involvement via Skype. Carolina asked if they had captured the suspects. He replied the limo was abandoned, but that there was a large search underway. He also acknowledged that because of her mentioning leaving on a jet to police earlier, they had temporarily grounded all private jet flights departing Denver International.

"The limo driver mentioned that a bicycle pulled out in front of him causing him to swerve. So did you find the cyclist?" Carolina directed the question to the inspector. He looked at her bewildered, and then shook his head, but before he could verbally respond, his phone buzzed.

"I see. Good! They've got the driver," the inspector announced to the occupants of the car, then directed a question to the presumed subordinate on the phone. "One more thing, the victim overheard the driver mention a bicyclist darting in front of the limo, which caused the crash. See what you can find out." He ended the call then focused back on Carolina.

"Don't worry, we'll find the other three assailants. I'm going to need you to stop by the police station to fill out more paper work and identify the driver. I'm sure that the *Post* will have you there anyway. I will need to be in contact periodically too, so be accessible." Carolina acknowledged, as the Inspector took another call, but this time there were very few words exchanged. He mostly just listened. The Inspector put his phone in his jacket pocket and turned back around to face his guests in the back seat.

"The driver is indeed emphatic that a female on a bicycle pulled in front of him, despite no other witness collaborating his story. Actually he was sure that he hit her. But, no cyclist, no body, no bent up bike. By the way, other witnesses reported one woman and three men running away from the scene. For the record and according to my men, you match the description of the fleeing woman," Inspector Miller stated.

"Well Miss Paige, this story lacks a motive. Can you shed any light on why these Colombian individuals would want to kidnap you?"

Before she could answer, Whitten interjected. "Ms. Paige just returned from assignment in Colombia. Our team at the *Post* will thoroughly review all information obtained from her trip and provide a formal report to your office."

Inspector Miller looked at Whitten suspiciously then replied. "I'm sure that you will, because you more that anyone should know that by law, even the press is not exempt from withholding evidence, especially, when a federal crime such as kidnapping has been committed.

Okay, we are done here." The inspector pointed to Bruce standing outside of the car, then looked directly at Whitten to conclude his lecture, "You also better keep your hired gun camped out in Ms. Paige's hip pocket until we bring this to a close."

Whitten nodded at the inspector as he and Carolina climbed out of the car. They joined Bruce, then proceeded to the helicopter for a quick flight back to the newspaper. No words were exchanged between the three until after they landed at the *Post* and sat down in Whitten's office.

CHAPTER 23

"I know, I know, it was very stupid of me to disobey Bruce and venture out on my own. And, I want to apologize to both of you," Carolina said.

"Yes well, I don't know whether to fire you or promote you. I'm afraid if I fire you, one of the local TV stations will snatch you up, so I guess that I'm stuck with you." Whitten showed a rare grin, and then continued, "Let's say that we are now even. I made a bone-headed decision to let you go alone to Bogotá and you made an equally stupid decision to head out here alone without Bruce. That's history now. We shouldn't dwell on our blunders, but learn from our mistakes. What we need to focus on now is this developing story."

"Carolina, you must have kicked a hornets' nest while you were in Bogotá. For the hornets to follow you back to Denver, you must have uncovered something really big and they feel threatened. There could be several tentacles to this story, drugs, weapons, prostitution, extortion, hell even collaborators to FARC. Whatever it is one of the tentacles have stretched has to Denver and to our Mayor Higgins. I need you to start from the beginning and tell me what happened after you left here today. I'll edit the official police statement later as well as a select piece regarding the kidnapping attempt for tomorrow's front page. Then we'll revisit and review in detail everything about your 'Colombian expedition,' including your FARC friend Diego. But first Bruce here wants to say a few words to you before he excuses himself from our meeting."

Even though there were only three of them in Whitten's office, Big Bruce felt the need to stand to deliver his speech. "Thanks Marty. Well I don't dismiss what happened earlier today as just a 'stupid or boneheaded decision', the bottom line is the *Post* hired me to keep you safe and I failed. So, things are going to ratchet up starting now. First of all, you are going to wear a tracking device twenty-four, seven." Bruce leaned over and pulled from his backpack what appeared to be a women's pendant necklace and handed it to Carolina. "Not exactly Tiffany's, but it ain't Wal-Mart either. I can track your ass around the globe by satellite from this device. However you won't be going around the globe unless it's with me. This charming little accent accessory will immediately send my phone an alarm if you get more than three hundred feet away from me. So put that around your neck and don't take it off! Secondly, I checked us into the Marriott under the assumed name, Mr. and Mrs. Bond."

"WHAT?" Carolina shot out of her chair like she was being launched from Cape Canaveral, and her voice projected with equal percussion, as she declared, "There's no way that I'm sharing a hotel room with, with a, who are you? Seriously, did you say James Bond?" Carolina turned to Whitten with her mouth open and her hands on her hips.

"Calm down. I've got us adjoining rooms and it's not James Bond, just Bond, our last name is Bond. Your apartment has been compromised. We have no other choice," Bruce retorted.

"I was abducted in the middle of the day in downtown Denver, not in my apartment! It was most likely them who broke into my hotel room in Bogotá's finest hotel too. If they did as you say 'compromise' my little apartment, that doesn't necessarily mean they will return, especially now. I don't think it's as much the location to these thugs as the opportunity." She turned and faced Whitten. "I will not let these assholes intimidate me and disrupt my life! Sir, as my boss if you want me to go into complete hiding by cowering in some hotel room under an assumed name, well then I guess that's what I'll do. But if you want me to do my job as a journalist for the largest news print organization in Denver, please let me retain some of my freedom. I have no problem with wearing the necklace, tracking device, or having Bruce as my shadow, but moving into a hotel room, well I just think that's surrendering to these thugs."

Carolina turned to Bruce. "Bruce, I'm sure that Mr. Kaleido will let you stay inside the store. There's a backroom, with a cot and you will be right below me."

Carolina stepped back and looked at both men, and then Whitten looked at Bruce. "What do you think Bruce? It's your call!"

Bruce took in a deep breath, puffed out his cheeks and then slowly released the spent air. "Okay, for the record, I'm not onboard with this but I'll look at the layout of the bicycle shop, and if I can tactically secure the environment and also have quick access to Ms. Paige..."

Carolina sensed a weakness and before he could finish his sentence she pounced on him like a lion on an unsuspecting gazelle. She grabbed the necklace and slipped it over her head, and then extended her arm inviting Bruce to a fist bump. "Okay big guy, it's a deal! I will be your obedient servant and you'll be my shadow. I will sleep safe and sound knowing that you will be right below me in the bicycle shop." Flirtatiously she sealed the deal with a wink, accompanied with a seductive smile, making it virtually impossible for him to renege on his assumed consent to stay in her apartment. Helpless and defeated, he smiled and fist bumped her back. Whitten chimed in with a couple of snarky comments regarding the unneeded drama, and then asked Bruce to relax in the lounge area while they do their work.

CHAPTER 24

Hours went by. The afternoon turned to evening, which turned into night. They fueled their laborious journalistic marathon with Chinese delivery, intercepted of course by Bruce, chased with pots of coffee. It was a scene of organized chaos with Carolina tapping out the chronicles of her saga on her laptop, Whitten pounding out tomorrow's morning headline on his, while making phone calls to his hired Colombian private investigators and trolling the internet for information.

After lots of bantering back and forth with Carolina, Whitten decided it would be prudent to let Inspector Miller know about Diego and his Skype appearance in the limousine. Details of some of his threatening rhetoric and allegations of FARC involvement would be omitted at this time. Whitten also decided to expose the childhood connection between Mayor Higgins and the late Mayor

Vargas, but their suspicions of improprieties at the Denver Homeless Coalition would also not be shared.

Whitten formatted the recent transgression to Carolina, but decided to stay with his original strategy and have Carolina go on the offense and try to call him, but not tonight. It was too soon.

Within forty eight minutes Whitten was ready to go to press with tomorrow's lead story and headline.

'FOILED KIDNAPPING OF OUR OWN JOURNALIST'

Yesterday our professional family here at the Denver Post was stunned to find out that one of our own journalists, Carolina Paige was abducted in the middle of the day in downtown Denver, and if that wasn't brazen enough by the abductors, it happened in front of the City County Building.

By God's grace the limousine used in the abduction was involved in an incident on, Route 25 allowing Ms. Paige to escape on foot.

The four male assailants were described by Paige as dark-skinned and Spanish speaking. The driver was captured at the scene and he is reported to be cooperating with authorities. It has been confirmed that he is a Colombian citizen holding an expired visa. The three other assailants fled on foot and are still at large. Neighborhoods in that area are under lock down and individual residential searches are underway.

Why Ms. Paige was targeted is still unclear at this time. She has just returned from a work-related trip to Bogotá, Colombia. Paige suffered minor injuries at the scene but reported back to work shortly afterward.

More articles will be forthcoming by Carolina Paige and our journalist team here at the Post.

Senor Editor, Martin Whitten

CHAPTER 25

As the sun was coming up, Bruce drove home an exhausted Carolina. Kaleidospokes was not open yet so Bruce did an inspection of her apartment and then retired back to his car at the curb.

Carolina fell asleep immediately, but once the morning edition hit the streets her cell phone lit up like a Christmas tree, waking her immediately. She was so exhausted after checking the messages of her first two calls, she silenced her phone.

An hour or so, later Bruce noticed movement in the store, and then the ceremonial flipping of the closed sign to the open side, followed by Karl retrieving the rolled up newspaper resting in front of the door. Within ten minutes the door flew open and Karl flew out, heading for the staircase to Carolina's apartment. Bruce immediately reacted.

"Mr. Kaleido, Sir!" Bruce shouted as he exited his vehicle. Karl turned to Bruce, and then pointed up to the second floor.

"Is she okay? I can't believe what I just read in the morning edition, "Karl's voice was strained by anxiety.

"She's fine Karl, she's just exhausted. The best thing for her now is sleep. Come on let's go inside and I'll bring you up to speed. Got any coffee in there?" Bruce walked over and put his hand on Karl's shoulder.

"I just started a pot, come on in, son," Karl looked up at Bruce and smiled. "I'll let her sleep, you keep her safe!"

They retreated to the back kitchen of the store. Karl pulled two cups from the cupboard and then poured them full with black coffee.

"Sugar's in the jar and creamer's in the fridge," Karl proclaimed.

"Black is my preference, thanks. Listen, I need to get back out front, but I really want to explain what happened to Carolina, and also ask you for a favor too. Do you mind sitting a while with me in the car?" Bruce asked.

"Of course not, and if the favor involves Carolina's safety, anything that I can help with, I will." Karl made a sweeping motion with his hand, indicating they should get back outside to Bruce's post, but responded to him as they walked toward the door. "I've only known Carolina for a short period of time, but it's as if I've know her all my life. She reminds me so much of someone I was very close to once upon a time. In fact, she lived in the same apartment that... I'm sorry, sometimes I babble on and on. I guess, Carolina's like the daughter that I never had and I feel like a surrogate father while she's staying in my place."

Bruce and Karl walked over and climbed into Bruce's car. As they sipped their coffee, Bruce explained in depth the threats that were made to Carolina that lead to his hiring, her abduction and escape. He also explained the dangers that still exist to her because of the assailants being at large. He was also clear that against his advice, Carolina insisted that she wanted to stay at her own apartment as opposed to a secret location. But to do this he must do a thorough inspection of the entire building and add security measures where needed. He would also like permission to bunk out somewhere inside the store. And of course Karl said 'yes', to all of his requests.

CHAPTER 26

U pstairs in her bed Carolina was thrashing around, kicking and convulsing, yet sound asleep. She was having one of her routine dreams, through the eyes of her mysterious cyclist friend.

"Elizabeth's in trouble! Elizabeth's needs help! WAKE UP! Wake up!" Suddenly Carolina was not dreaming, she was being summoned by her friend. The bed shook and Carolina sat straight up and shouted, "Elizabeth!" She then turned to her phone on the night stand which was lit up, showing messages and missed calls. Immediately she exited her bed and grabbed her phone. She had eleven missed calls and eight new messages. Panicked, Carolina looked at her clock on the nightstand which revealed late afternoon. She began scrolling through her missed calls and mentally segregating them by importance. It was her new phone issued by the *Post,* so there were only a limited number of people who had her new number. Suddenly there was a number she didn't recognize. It wasn't a family member, a friend, or a co-worker. She kept scrolling and there it was again. She switched to her messages and saw that number with an attached video. She opened it and gasped with horror.

There they were her three abductors from the other day! It appeared they were in the living room of someone's home. In the middle of the room was a blood-soaked figure tied in a chair. Hovering from behind was another figure, lifeless and dangling from a noose. The video zoomed in to the person in the chair. It was Elisabeth. Thin lines of blood and tears streamed down her face. Her mouth was taped shut, and her blood-red eyes were wide with terror. Carolina watched, crying and screaming as one of the thugs walked up to her and plunged a syringe into her arm. Then the gruesome video ended. Carolina noticed another text from this number, not with a video, but with a long sentence written in Spanish.

Carolina ran to her door, then out on her landing and waved and screamed for Bruce. She then dialed 911. It was a frustrating call because she had no idea where Elizabeth lived and it was a nightmare trying to explain the situation to the dispatch operator. Bruce arrived in seconds. Not knowing the situation, he barged through her door with his silver-plated Beretta extended. After a quick inspection of the premises he returned to the landing joining Karl cradling a hysterical Carolina. He took the phone from Carolina's hands and resumed conversing with the dispatcher. Listening to a mix of Carolina's quivering voice explaining what had happened and Karl's interpretation of what occurred in one ear and the dispatcher in the other he quickly determined he needed to call back. Bruce guided the two back inside and took a quick scan of the interior then joined them.

"I'm sorry Bruce, that was not very professional of me. I need to get a grip." Carolina wiped the tears from her eyes and took in a deep breath while pulling up her text message on her phone.

"Here, I woke up to this." She pushed play and handed the phone to Bruce.

"Meet the three goons who abducted me yesterday and that poor couple in the background are the Sanders, James and Elizabeth." Carolina's voice cracked. "Until yesterday Elizabeth worked for the Denver Homeless Coalition. I just interviewed her after her resignation. Well, assumed resignation, she was so upset, I'm not sure that she told the mayor. Oh my God, our lunch yesterday probably led to her murder," Carolina starting sobbing.

Bruce finished watching the video then handed the phone back to Carolina.

"Shut this off and don't use it, they've got your number again. Did you give Elizabeth your number?" Bruce asked. "Come on! We are heading to the police station. I'll call Inspector Miller and Whitten on the way. Karl, please lock up and if you have a gun, I suggest you find it."

Carolina ran into her bathroom, brushed her teeth, splashed water on her face, and threw on some jeans, a shirt and a ball cap. Meanwhile in the other room, Bruce was on the phone with Whitten. When she emerged Bruce grabbed her arm and quickly escorted her to his car. As they passed by Karl, Carolina hesitated and gave him a concerned stare.

"Don't worry, Missy. The boys and I will be fine!" Karl winked at her and then looked at Bruce. "I'll be breaking out more than just bicycle tools. You keep my Bec." Karl caught himself before finishing the name. "Keep my gal safe!"

As his car sped away Bruce relayed his conversation to Carolina. "Whitten said he would call the FBI's Inspector Miller and meet us at the police station. I wasn't able to translate the text or the audio on the video, but I don't think they killed Elizabeth. It looked like they were giving her a sedative to knock her out, probably to transport her."

"I need your phone, Bruce! The Mayor's office is still open. I will call Higgins' secretary, she can get me Elizabeth's address, every second counts. We'll have it for the police when we arrive."

Bruce handed her his phone and she when to work.

Carolina lived twenty minutes from the Denver Police Station and it took her eighteen minutes to retrieve the Sander's address. She didn't want to alert the receptionist to the ominous events, knowing it would obviously tip off Higgins.

She skillfully navigated around the privacy law by telling the receptionist that she had promised to return Elizabeth's apple cobbler dish by the end of the day, but she had accidently lost the address. As fate would have it, the receptionist was also a fan of Elizabeth's cobbler and was empathetic to Carolina's fabricated story and within a couple of clicks and scrolls on her computer she had Elizabeth's address and shared it with Carolina.

They pulled into the police parking lot, shut the car off and ran toward the entrance. At the door Carolina waved her press credentials at one the guards and explained it was a life or death emergency. He escorted her past the front desk and to a detective's office. Within seconds the initial questioning was taken and police units were dispatched.

Carolina pulled out the card of the sergeant who interviewed her at the scene of the botched kidnapping and handed it to the detective, while giving him an abbreviated version of her abduction saga. Bruce also informed him of the imminent arrival of Inspector Miller of the FBI and her boss Whitten.

As soon as he finished his sentence, Bruce saw Whitten through the glass door, being escorted to their location. Whitten stepped in the office and Bruce stepped out. Soon they were joined by the investigating officer, then Miller and the big guns from the FBI. Quick introductions were made. Then the crowd moved to a larger room. Bruce turned on Carolina's phone and handed it to her to retrieve the video from her text messages. She then handed it to Miller.

The detective approached Miller and reached out his hand. "May I?" Miller handed him the phone and with some assistance from Carolina they transferred the video from her phone to the flat screen on the wall. The room was silent as they watched the graphic video twice.

The second time pausing and magnifying at different intervals. Carolina looked away. She even left the room at one point. Even though the lighting was poor and some parts out of focus, she could not bear to watch again. Her formal education and internship did not prepare her for this horror. While the detectives and agents took notes, dissected and analyzed, Miller took Carolina and Whitten back to the original office so they could talk.

"Whitten, I got your thoughtful and guarded account of the events leading up to Ms. Paige's abduction in my inbox. But when I read it, I couldn't help but feel there must be something else that happened while your reporter was in Colombia that perhaps got omitted from your synopsis. Then it occurred to me, it was not your reporter, Carolina Paige who wrote this, it was you. Perhaps something was omitted, let's just say, got lost in the translation." Miller's sarcasm was enforced by the tone in his voice. "Listen, I understand that the *Post* may be conducting their own investigation of something and that you may feel reluctant to share everything in fear of jeopardizing your story. I need to know what that 'something' is! I am not the Denver or for that matter any other city or state police agency where things aren't always kept on the lock down. I am the Federal Bureau of Investigation and I… we don't leak our investigations to the media."

"So Mr. Whitten, I'm sure that you won't mind if this time I conduct my own interview with Ms. Paige, alone! Is the *Denver Post* ready to tell me the rest of the story?" Before Whitten could respond to the inspector's stern query the door opened and the detective walked into the room.

"The homicide was confirmed by the responding police units. One male, late 60's, the preliminary report at the scene was death by strangulation, a hanging as we saw on the video."

"What about Elizabeth? Was there a female at the scene?" Carolina frantically asked.

"Negative." Responded the detective.

Carolina turned away and put her hands over her face.

The previously stoic Whitten spoke up, "Paige, cooperate with inspector Miller!"

Whitten walked to the door, stopped then turned around to face Miller.

"I assume that you're done with me. And you won't mind if I follow your agents to the crime scene."

"The freedom of the press, Mr. Whitten, you don't need my approval. But you know that." Whitten said nothing, before exiting the room. Miller turned to Carolina and said, "Are you ready to get started Ms. Paige?" Miller pointed toward the rectangular table with two chairs. Carolina nodded then took her place.

"Sir, before we start, can I ask? I'm a little rusty with my Spanish/Colombian dialect and was only able to translate a few words from the video and nothing from the text. I haven't had an opportunity to check with our team at the *Post* regarding the precise translation. Can you interpret for me?"

"Are you familiar with FARC?"

"Yes, unfortunately that was one of the few words I was able to translate." Carolina answered.

"FARC, just another wonderful byproduct of our porous Southern Border. It's not just Islamic Terrorists flooding our Country, it's drug cartels and guerrilla forces from South America." Miller digressed, but quickly got back on subject.

"Obviously, I have not gotten a complete and accurate vernacular translation yet; however what I was able to quickly interpret with the audio was that their allegiance was to the Fuerzas Armadas Revolucionarias de Colombia Revolutionary, English translation, Armed Forces OF Colombia, or FARC. Lots of propaganda and verbal threats. The written text was more organized and intentional. It basically stated that they were taking Mrs. Sanders back to Colombia and would hold her until you turned yourself over to Colombian authorities in Bogotá. They believe you are responsible for the murder of Mayor Luis Francisco Vargas. Once you've surrendered, they will release Mrs. Sanders unharmed. The author of the text also mentioned something about stealing State secrets. That reminds me, please excuse me, I need to confirm something." Miller stood up and left the room, then returned in ten minutes later.

"Sorry, I had a hunch that I needed to confirm. The cell phone that was used at the scene to video the crime as well as texted you were still at the scene and it was registered to Elizabeth Sanders. I assume that you left her your cell phone number."

"Yes, at the conclusion of our coffee the other day." Carolina shook her bowed head in shame. "I can't believe this is happening! What have I done?"

"Listen, forget about what has been done or not done and work with me on what needs to happen to get these savages. I will need your complete cooperation, I mean I will need for you to set aside your journalistic code of principles or whatever you news folks align with and cooperate with the FBI. You'll get your story, but it will be at the end of the journey and after justice is served!"

Carolina looked at Miller and said, "Let's get started!"

She began to chronicle her account starting from the beginning and omitting nothing, including what Elizabeth divulged to her at their lunch. She showed him the copy of the Polaroid of a young Higgins and Vargas. She shared the letter from Mayor Vargas to her, announcing his death and exonerating her of the crime of murder. Miller kept her documents to give to his lab to study the authenticity.

Other than a couple of clarifications Inspector Miller let Carolina speak uninterrupted. When she concluded he asked her two questions.

"So Ms. Paige, this is off the record and you may choose not to respond but, in your journalistic opinion, what do you think is going on here? Also, why do you think Diego Morales or FARC are so threatened by you that they are willing to come to the States to kidnap or threaten you?"

"In regards to your first question, I believe there has been some sort of illicit business relationship between Diego, Mayor Vargas and the Denver Homeless Coalition and perhaps our Mayor Higgins, Diego basically admitted it in his Skype visit in the limousine. I believe that extortion may have been used to coerce one or both of the mayors. As far as the second question, I think that Diego believes that Vargas shared something with me before his death that will devastate his business. However, I don't know what imprisoning me would accomplish. What was the point of killing an innocent James Sanders? Why didn't they just kill me?

"Inspector Miller, We must hurry and save Elizabeth! I am ready to go back to Bogotá, if need be. I am willing to do whatever must be done to spare her life."

"Carolina, I will need your help, but right now I need you to hold tight. The FBI with the assistance of the Denver Police and Colorado State Police need time to compile all the evidence. We do understand the urgency, I assure you. As with all fleeing kidnapping or murder suspects, time is of the essence. Immediately after your arrival here a mass A.P.B. was issued to numerous law enforcement agencies throughout Colorado and surrounding states, which includes TSA and ICE. And, in this case, because they announced their intent to go to Colombia, I extended the bulletin to include all the Border States. We have also sent a wire to the Mexican authorities to be on the lookout for one to three Colombian men traveling with a Caucasian woman in her mid to late sixty's. Once we receive a recent photo of her, we will attach and update. Denver Police will also release the photo to the local television newscasts along with a report."

"If indeed they are heading back to Colombia by vehicle they have most likely already crossed the southern border. Of course if they somehow manage to fly, they would already be in Bogotá, but I highly doubt it. After your abduction we alerted TSA about our Colombian friends' desire to fly private. I subsequently grounded all private charters from all Colorado Airports to Colombia. My agents have been pouring over manifests of all charter companies, their destinations and passengers and so far we have come up with nothing. It's highly unlikely that our Colombian abductors and guest are flying commercial. Flight attendants would question the blindfold and duct tape. Sorry, that comment was inappropriate," Miller grimaced then continued.

"I'm not totally convinced that they are taking her to Colombia. It just doesn't seem prudent. They want you in Bogotá of course, but what is the necessity to have Elizabeth there? She can be a hostage here in Denver just as well as in Bogotá.

"As far as Diego's interest in you, I'm still mulling that over as well.

"We are doing all we can until we obtain more solid evidence. Right now, I'm going to the crime scene. I'm keeping your phone; in fact I need to rush this off to the lab. It seems that we are starting a collection of your compromised cell phones." Miller smiled. "Whitten gave me your other one just the other day. I suspect they will try and contact you now that they have your number. At least I hope that they do, because we'll be right there to trace their call."

"Ms. Paige, go with Bruce, lay low for a while and I will meet you and your boss at the *Post* later." Miller walked over to the door and opened it for Carolina. Bruce was in the hall leaning against the far wall. When he saw them exiting he stood up. Inspector Miller repeated the same instructions to him, but also informed them that the Denver Police would be adding twenty-four hour surveillance at the *Post* and at the bicycle shop.

CHAPTER 27

They did as the inspector requested and returned to Carolina's apartment.

When Bruce pulled up to the curb and before their doors opened Karl was there to greet them. Holstered visibly around Karl's hip was his second amendment right.

"The boys and I have been getting you a place to sleep," Karl voiced to Bruce as he walked around the car to join him, but then he turned his attention to Carolina.

"I've made some ice tea," Karl nodded toward his door, indicating an invitation.

"Sure! Tea sounds wonderful and just what I need!" Bruce nodded in agreement. "So Karl, it looks like you're the new sheriff of Kaleidospokes." Carolina pointed to his firearm and smiled, and Karl winked back.

It was past store hours, but despite the closed sign on the door the inside of the store was a bustle. The mechanics were doing various things but all stopped to greet Carolina as she entered the building.

Karl motioned to them and they dropped what they were doing and quickly formed a line.

"Bruce, I recognize that despite your brief encounter at the base of Carolina's stairs the other day, you've never been formally introduced to the boys. Today, I want you to meet your men! While you are here they are at your disposal. I realize they're not exactly a full-fledged militia, but they're not a group of bungling buffoons either." The four young men stood at attention while a bemused Bruce and Carolina stood speechless. Suddenly Karl barked out an order and the four young men scrambled to different parts of the store, then returned with weaponry a bit upgraded from the other day. All were lined up sporting a combination of long rifles or shotguns.

"I don't know what to say, Karl," Bruce suddenly broke his silence.

Karl walked over to his newly formed soldiers and introduced each to Bruce.

"Well now that you've been formally introduced, I'll leave you to get more familiar with each other. Guys show Mr. Watt where he will be bunking. Carolina, make yourself at home. I will fetch the tea from the kitchen."

Karl spoke out to one specific boy who was acting as the group leader.

"Carlton, show Mr. Bruce the abandoned laundry chute which leads to Carolina's apartment. He may want to run wires for video or listening devices through there."

Carolina immediately interjected.

"Video or listening devices? I don't think so! That's NOT going to happen! I'm already wearing this gaudy tracking necklace that looks like it came right off of some femme fatale." Carolina looked sternly at Bruce, for which he responded by shaking his head and gestured a shrug with his arms.

"Karl, may I give you a hand in the kitchen?" Carolina walked over closer to Mr. Kaleido so that she could speak in a softer tone.

"I was hoping that I could talk to you about something in private."

"Of course you can Sweetheart!" Karl put his hand on Carolina's shoulder directing her toward the kitchen and they walked away leaving Bruce to deal with his new army of bicycle mechanics. He waited for Karl and Carolina to be gone from sight before addressing his eager troops.

"Guys I appreciate your boss' eagerness to help by drafting you into service. I'm sure that being a bodyguard wasn't part of your job description when you were hired. At this time, I really don't need an armed militia. However, it's good to know that I can count on you for back up if needed. All I really need from you is to step up your awareness. Be vigilant, but go about your normal daily activities as if nothing is wrong. And really, nothing is wrong. The thugs who tried to abduct Carolina are probably thousands of miles away. However just as a precaution, the Denver Police have stepped up surveillance twenty-four/seven on this building and as you know the *Denver Post* has hired me to personally guard Ms. Paige. I have more than twenty years in law enforcement experience, most of which I spent with the Secret Service.

"So if you guys are good with that, how about you show me my new digs, that is, after you first go and put away those hunting rifle's and shotguns." The relieved group of young volunteers were grateful to hear Bruce's expectation.

Karl opened the refrigerator and grabbed the pitcher of iced tea and gestured to Carolina to sit at the small table. He set the pitcher on the table beside the already present glasses then retrieved the ice from the freezer. After filling three glasses with ice he returned the container to the freezer and joined Carolina at the table.

"What's on your mind, Missy?" Karl poured two tall glasses of tea and waited for Carolina's response. It was obvious to Karl that she was having difficulty with starting her conversation. "Just spit it out Girl! Nobody ever died from a Karl Kaleido bite!"

"I'm supposed to be the professional journalist in the room, but I'm having a hard time formulating a question in the fashion that you won't subsequently think that I'm crazy. I also promised myself that with my friends and family I would never delve into their personal affairs unless invited. So I'm about to break that promise and I hope that you don't think that I'm certifiable when I'm through."

Karl leaned forward and reached across the table grabbing Carolina's hands. "It's okay! In fact, I am delighted to hear that you think of me as a friend! So ask!"

"Karl, because I rushed off before, we never got a chance to finish our conversation about your fiancée Rebecca and it's been bothering me."

"What do you mean? Who has been bothering you?" he asked. That was the fire that lit Carolina's fuse.

"REBECCA!" Carolina elevated her voice. "The girl whose bike is hanging in your store! The girl that I've been having dreams about ever since I moved in upstairs! The girl who's been haunting me and stalking me!" Carolina's voice faded to almost a whisper. "And it seems, even protecting me. Tell me Karl, who is this girl for whom you've mistakenly called me twice? Karl, I need to know who Becky is and I need to know why she is doing this! I need for you to tell me that I'm not going crazy."

Karl released Carolina's hands then recoiled back in his chair. His mouth immediately gaped opened as it was vividly apparent he was having difficulty processing what Carolina had just unloaded on him. The look on his face was of sorrowful disbelief and he began to tremble.

"My God, I don't know what has come over me. Once I started I couldn't stop. I am sorry! Are you okay?" Carolina could see that he wasn't reacting to her questions well. "I am sorry Sir, you don't…"

Karl interrupted. "Deary, there is no need to apologize! You are not crazy! I believe you when you say that you can see my Rebecca. It just seems surreal to hear you say it. There are times when I see her too, well at least visions or glimpses of light or shadows that I believe to be Becky. Actually, not a day goes by here at the store when I don't feel someone next to me. There have been times when I have been here alone at night and I hear a faint whisper in my ear." He paused a moment reflecting. "There have also been times when I've looked at you, but it is Becky who I see," Karl chuckled. "Now who's the crazy one?"

"You know, you are staying in Rebecca's room. My father years ago rented the apartment upstairs. She was the first and the only occupant of that room, until you arrived. After she tragically passed, the room was vacant for years. Even after I inherited the business, the room remained empty. I just couldn't deal with someone else living there."

"I remember boxing up her belongings to ship to her sister in Iowa and wondering how I was going to ship the racing bike. Becky had two bikes, one that she rode daily around here and the racing bike, the one that's hanging in the showroom. That bike was her prized possession and she kept it in the apartment. Becky had it against the wall with the wheels up, as not to cause flat spots on the rubber tires."

"I was sitting on her bed and looked over and asked that inanimate object, 'So, what am I going to do with you?' And, as if it were responding to my question, the wheels began slowly spinning. Needless to say, I was finished; I jumped up, grabbed the remaining two boxes, pulled the door closed and flew down stairs, but left the bike. It was two years after that before I could find the courage to even set foot back inside."

"Then a few years after that, I finally had a plaque engraved with a response she made to a question from a member of the press, just after her cross country journey. Both the plaque and the bike are still displayed where you see them today."

"What was the question from the reporter?" Carolina asked.

"Something like, '*being a women and alone, you must have been very frightened at times.*' This provoked a quick response from Becky, 'I WAS NEVER AFRAID.' Those four words headlined her story in newspapers and cycling magazines around the world."

Karl paused and took a drink of ice tea, smiled then finished his thought. "And, she wasn't either! Never afraid, that is."

"Why is she haunting me, Karl? What does she want me to do?"

"I don't know, Missy, why don't you ask her?"

Carolina was struck speechless. For several seconds the kitchen was quiet as both Carolina and Karl drifted in thought. But, that would soon end as Bruce bolted into the room.

"Whitten just called, Inspector Miller wants us back down at the *Post!*" Carolina looked away momentarily to acknowledge Bruce, then redirected her focus back to Karl.

"I need to ask you one more thing Karl. Was Rebecca an acquaintance of Luis Vargas the Mayor of Bogotá?" Karl immediately looked startled by Carolina's question.

"What do you mean? Of course not, why do you ask? As you know, Becky was planning her bicycle trek though Colombia and we were planning to be married in Bogotá, but she never made it. She never even set foot anywhere south of the U.S. border."

"No, no, I am sorry! She would have met Vargas long before he was the mayor of Bogotá. She or for that fact you could have possibly met Luis as a teenager. It seems he was an exchange student here in Denver in 1966 and 1967. Actually his high school was only a few blocks for here.

"The reason I'm asking is that in Mayor Vargas's letter to me, perhaps his final letter before killing himself, he mentions your Becky. When I was in Bogotá he also saw a vision of her. More specifically, he thought that I was

Becky. My assessment; he was extremely stricken by guilt for something and he had been carrying the burden of this remorse for years."

"Karl, I think Luis Vargas was involved in Rebecca's death!"

Carolina hopped out of her chair and went around the table and gave Karl a hug.

"Here we go again; it seems we can never finish our chat. Next time, I want to find out more about Rebecca, her childhood, your relationship with her and of course, I want to learn more about your recollection of the details of her passing."

Karl sat rigid and without emotion staring into space as Carolina hesitated at the doorway for a moment waiting for a response which never came. Once he heard the door shut, he guzzled down the rest of his tea then buried his head into his hands on the table.

CHAPTER 28

B ruce and Carolina arrived at the *Post* and joined Whitten, Inspector Miller and another FBI agent in the conference room. Bruce initially stopped at the door, but Miller motioned him to come in the room, saying he should from now on be a part of their meetings.

On the long table was a scrambled mess of wires and a black box which looked like a VCR recorder. On top of this box and plugged into the device was a phone.

"He tried to call you." Whitten blurted out before Carolina and Bruce had a chance to sit.

Inspector Miller gave Whitten a look of disapproval at his outburst. "Actually your friend Diego tried to get in touch with you on two different occasions. Both calls were within a couple of hours after the video texts were sent to your phone. He left no messages. I would surmise that his henchmen thugs found your number at the Sanders home, called back to Diego, probably giving Diego the idea to video the crime and try to terrorize you into turning yourself over to them. I guess that he was just following up to see how his plan was working," Miller continued, "We were unable to trace either call from either phone. Doesn't matter, I speculate that he's in Bogotá anyway. Apprehending Diego at this point is of no value to us. We need to first find the thugs who abducted Mrs. Sanders and of course find Mrs. Sanders, assuming she's still alive."

"Mr. Whitten you indicated earlier that the *Denver Post* would cooperate fully with our investigation, is that still the case?"

"Absolutely!" Whitten belted out.

"Ms. Paige, you as well indicated that you personally would cooperate completely and unambiguously with the FBI, is that still your intention?"

"What the hell do you think, Columbo?" Carolina angrily snapped back. "I believe I was very clear when I said that I was prepared to do whatever was needed to help free Elizabeth and kill those bastards who abducted her and killed James!"

"Are you, Ms. Paige? Because no one said anything about killing these perpetrators! If you are going to help us, you need to keep your composure. I very much need your help. But, I need for you to set aside your anger and cooperate with us in a profession manner or we can forget about finding Elizabeth alive, or capturing her assailants. So I ask you again, Ms Paige, will you cooperate completely with the FBI?"

Carolina humbly nodded after Miller's lecture and then responded. "I'm sorry Inspector. For the record, I am fully aware of what is at stake here. I will, Sir. I will check my anger and completely cooperate with you. So, what do you need me to do?"

"I want you to try and make contact with him. I want you to call him, but not on your cell phone. He's not an idiot, I'm sure that he knows your phone is in police custody. A call from your cell he would either not answer or he would answer but be very guarded as to what he would say. Actually, he probably will not answer your call, mainly because he won't recognize the number, so you'll leave a brief and concise message, and then wait for his return."

"You need to try and convince him that you need to talk with him to try and clear your name. Which by the way and contrary to the rumors on the streets of Bogotá, no formal charges have been filed against you for your involvement in the murder of Mayor Vargas, at least not yet. As obvious as this sounds, I want you to plead for the release of Elizabeth Sanders. Plead, not demand, right now you are in no position to make demands. Your pleading will show vulnerability and hopefully make him think that he has control over you. *This is very important.* You need to tell him that you do not trust the Colorado authorities with the safety of Mrs. Sanders! Tell Diego that they have warned you of going back to Bogotá and have put you on a twenty four hour watch, making it impossible to leave Denver. If he asks, tell him that you're making this call from a friend's house, because they confiscated your phone. We need to force his hand to agree to send his men to come and get you. If Elizabeth Sanders is the bait for your swap, then tell Diego that he needs to instruct them to bring her in order to get you."

"Tell Diego that you need to talk to Mrs. Sanders to verify that she's safe, before this trade happens. As I said before, I think the thugs are still in the U.S. possibly still in Colorado. We need for them to call you back at this number," Miller pointed to the phone.

"Yes, I get it!" Carolina confirmed.

"You know, it's a bit ingenious for me to refer to the assailants as 'thugs' this would lead one to believe that they are common gang members when actual they are a ruthless militia of killers. They are FARC!" Miller stated.

"Yes FARC. Besides his false accusation of murder, how arrogant and impetuous it was for Diego to add to my resume that I, 'the female *Denver Post* journalist' was a FARC sympathizer." Carolina opined. "So, Inspector what are we waiting for? Let's make the call!"

Miller looked at Whitten, and then Bruce. They both nodded their heads in approval, so he looked back at Carolina.

"Okay then, let's make the call. Remember, it's okay to sound nervous and scared, but don't worry about winning an academy award!"

Carolina acknowledged. "Are you all set Gonzalez?" Miller's question was directed to his agent, who was now wearing earphones. The agent responded with a thumbs-up sign, and then switched on the black box. Miller reached over and picked up the receiver and handed it to Carolina. He then slipped on his pair of headphones and Gonzalez dialed the phone.

RING! RING! RING! The phone rang several times and as predicted no one answered. Finally, there was a long tone indicating the recording had begun, but no voice.

"Diego, it's Carolina Paige, I'm at a friend's house using their phone. Please give me a call at this number; I desperately need to talk to you! I will be waiting." Miller slid over a piece of paper with the phone number written on it and she clearly recited it. When she finished, Gonzalez hung up.

"Well done! Now we wait," Miller announced.

And, wait they did. Minutes went by, turning into hours, but no call. They took turns pacing the room and making small talk. When it was Miller's turn, he made one circle around the table, before sharing a couple of relevant things with the group.

"Just so you know, ICE has confirmed that the limo driver's visa expired six years ago. He also had an invalid chauffer's license too. So to reward him for his criminal behavior, they have ordered us to release him from custody, so that they can deport him back to Colombia." Miller's disgust was obvious.

"On a more productive note, I have also opened a subsequent investigation of the Denver Homeless Coalition. If there's been inappropriate money-funneling in or out of the commission, or transactions with Diego Morales, Mayor Vargas, or FARC we'll find out."

Carolina responded with a snide comment saying, "I thought the FBI never leaked their investigations to the press." Whitten was the only one who was amused.

Suddenly there was a ring, more like a buzz, it wasn't the phone in the middle of the table, it was Bruce's phone in his pocket. He pulled it out and looked at it and declared, "It's the bicycle shop!" He looked at Miller. "Shall I answer?" Miller, answered, "Yes but make it quick!"

"Hello?"

"Mr. Watt, this is Karl Kaleido. I just got a call from a frantic woman wanting to talk with Carolina. She said that her name was Elizabeth! I asked for her number so that Carolina could call her back, but she said she couldn't give it to me. Bruce, she said that she would call back in exactly thirty minutes and if Carolina didn't answer, the men would kill her!"

"Karl we are on our way." Bruce looked at Whitten. "We got to go! They just had Elizabeth call the bicycle shop for Carolina. She told Karl that they would call back in thirty minutes and Carolina had better answer."

"Gonzalez, we are taking our show on the road," Miller barked at his agent to bug out and he hurriedly started disconnecting lines. "We will head over there and agent Gonzalez will catch up. I estimate that ten of the thirty minutes have been burned up just between calls, so that only leaves us with twenty minutes and it's a twenty minute commute, normally. Let's pray my siren and lights will gain me at least five minutes!" They ran to the stairs, bypassing the slower elevators and scurried down the steps and into the parking lot. All four jumped into Miller's sedan, and within seconds they were flying down the street with siren blaring and headlights flashing. Whitten and Carolina were terrorized, their eyes as wide as silver dollars. Bruce was a bit more subdued, having made numerous high speed vehicle pursuits himself over his law enforcement career. He monitored the time and informed Miller of their progress every few blocks.

CHAPTER 29

When they arrived at Kaleidospokes they had about four minutes to spare. This was enough time for Carolina to retrieve Elizabeth's call, but unless he arrived very soon, not enough time for Agent Gonzalez to hook up the tracing gear.

Karl held the front door open while Carolina, Whitten and the Inspector hurried through. Karl then escorted the group to his office behind the counter and motioned for Carolina to take a seat in front of the phone.

"I apologize, I only have one land line," Karl declared.

Bruce filed back to the door to watch for Gonzales, while Inspector Miller continued to prepare Carolina for possible scenarios resulting from the call.

Miller checked his watch and determined that they had one minute. In the background they could hear the faint sound of a siren announcing the arrival of

Gonzales. Bruce walked out on the sidewalk to flag down the agent while Karl corralled his mechanics in the backroom. As Miller predicted it was too late to hook up the tracing equipment. When the bell on the door jingled announcing Bruce and Gonzales entering the shop, the phone rang.

Miller nodded at Carolina signaling her to pick up the phone.

"Hello."

On the other end it was indeed Elizabeth. She was sobbing and barely understandable. It was apparent that she wasn't cooperating with her captors. Carolina could hear her being coerced by an authoritarian voice in the background and over the phone she could hear breathing indicating that there was at least one other person on the line.

"Elizabeth!" Carolina shouted. "Please do as they say, I am going to get you out of there."

Elizabeth shouted back. "NO! DO NOT COOPERATE WITH THESE PIGS!" That warning statement by Elizabeth did not please her abductors and concluded her time on the phone. Miller who was now sitting next to Carolina leaned in close and they could hear clearly the thump of a falling phone receiver and the presumed dragging of Elizabeth off her chair and to the ground.

Numerous dull thuds and the unmistakable sickening sound of slapping of skin were too unbearable for Carolina. She went off script and began screaming on the phone. "STOP IT, YOU BASTARDS! LEAVE HER ALONE! She is innocent, release her immediately, or I will not cooperate! Diego, I know that you are listening. If you don't release her now I will have the *Denver Post* start printing every little dark pathetic secret that Luis has shared with me. You will be destroyed!"

Suddenly on the other end of the phone came the sound of clapping, followed by a familiar voice. It was Diego. "Bravo, Senorita Paige, you play your hand very well! Unfortunately your threats do little to alter my objective."

"Your objective?" Carolina screamed. "What kind of beast are you, if your objective is to kidnap torture and murder innocent people?"

"My associates' methods can be over exuberant at times, but their results are very effective."

"It is my objective to serve justice by bringing you back to Bogotá, to be judged for the untimely death of Mayor

Luis Vargas and return items in your possession which do not belong to you."

"That's absurd! There is absolutely no evidence that would support your claim and besides there have not been any charges brought against me by your local police or by Colombian Police. Regardless, your twisted form of jurisprudence is not justified in any shape or form. We have laws here in the United States with proper avenues and channels through our State Department to retrieve suspects. Your sending of murderous thugs to get your revenge is criminal and you know that!"

"You are sadly mistaken Senorita, it is not the city of Bogotá or the country of Colombia that I represent. My allegiance is and has always been to FARC."

Carolina looked up at Agent Miller and he gestured her to keep talking. "I really don't care who your twisted allegiance is with. As far as I'm concerned it's with Satan. I need for you to release Mrs. Sanders immediately. I can try to meet with you or your thugs, but it has to be somewhere here in Colorado. Returning to Bogotá is out of the question. They have me heavily guarded and I cannot go anywhere without an entourage of bodyguards. It may not be possible to meet here either, I don't know, but at least it's feasible whereas leaving the country is impossible. As we speak, they are outside of the room that I'm in and outside of the house."

"Of course Diego, there is the obvious. I'm talking to you now, just you and I, so why don't you ask me what you want right now?" Miller reached over and tapped Carolina on the shoulder, giving her a stern look and shaking his head no. He didn't think Diego would buy that and was relieved to hear his response.

"You insult my intelligence, you perra! What fool do you think that I am? I know that the police are listening to our conversation. I know that your previous call and recorded message to one of my phones was scripted, with the intent of tracing my location. I also know that you have the ability to do as you wish, you are not being incarcerated. So figure it out. I don't care how you get here, but you have twenty-four hours to physically make it to Bogotá or your friend Elizabeth dies! Also if you decide that she isn't worthy of you traveling here, we will keep eliminating your friends one-by-one until we find one who is. By the way, I had a wonderful conversation earlier with that old man from the bicycle shop. I can't wait to introduce him to my associates!"

"So this is the last time I will be talking to you over the phone. I better be talking to you face-to-face tomorrow or Elizabeth's blood will flow!" The phone went silent.

Miller stood up and looked at Agent Gonzales, then pointed to the phone. Despite not being connected to his black box, Gonzales had already anticipated what needed to be done and was working diligently toward getting a trace through dated and less technology-savvy resources at the FBI.

"I'm going to Bogotá!" Carolina blurted out, prompting Whitten and Miller to start to speak simultaneously, but before either could respond she continued, "We have no choice! You can fire me Mr. Whitten, and Inspector you know you cannot detain me." She paused a moment, then repeated, "We have no choice."

Gonzales lowered his cell phone from his ear and shook his head at Miller. Miller then responded to Carolina, "The wire trace was unsuccessful. Ms. Paige, you are mistaken. I can detain you indefinitely if I wish, declaring you as obstruction and a threat to an ongoing investigation. Here's a news flash, journalist lady, and I'm not going to soften it like I did earlier. They have no inclination of releasing Mrs. Sanders alive unless they have to. You run off to Colombia, I cannot assure your safety, and then I'll have two dead women on my hands. We are scouring every square foot of Colorado using the resources of literally every law enforcement agency in the state, including Game Wardens and Conservation Officers. All states from here to the border continue in high alert, but my hunch still remains the same, that they are held up somewhere within one hundred miles from here."

Whitten chimed in, "What about the Colombian government, surely they can be of assistance?"

"Dealing with Colombian authorities has never resulted favorably for the FBI, for that matter any U.S. departments. However it is protocol for me to contact the U.S. State Department as well as the appropriate Colombian law enforcement agencies to share all evidence and allegations against Bogotá's Mayor Vargas. It has also been our history that once we share information it makes it virtually impossible for us to retrieve the assailants. As far as the thugs here in the States, it's a catch and release program. We arrest and the government instructs us to release. Once they are processed they will automatically receive political immunity, and then be deported, probably to return in six months."

"Ms. Paige, please trust me. The best way you can help get Elizabeth Sanders back is to use your resources. Use your platform. Use the *Post*! Someone out there has had to see something."

Whitten responded for Elizabeth and himself, "Yes, tomorrow's front page and headline will carry this story. We'll have descriptions and sketches of the assailants. I will also share this information to the three local television newscasts, and as Carolina knows, that's something I rarely do. Of course I promise you that there won't be any mention of Mayor Higgins or the late Mayor Vargas, FARC or anything that would jeopardize this case. Are you with me Carolina? I need you to write this. It will be you first article since your abduction."

Carolina lowered her head and muttered, "Yes."

"Good!" Miller announced. We all have a lot of work to do, so Gonzales and I will be leaving. Oh, there is one more thing you can do for us Carolina that would be a tremendous help."

"What is that Inspector?"

"PRAY!" It always helps! Miller smiled as he and Gonzales exited.

"We have a lot of work to do as well, Paige! Come on Bruce, drive us back to the *Post*."

Carolina hugged Karl followed by Whitten and Bruce thanking him, then the three climbed back into Bruce's car and headed back to the Post for a long night of work.

CHAPTER 30

*T*HE DENVER ABDUCTIONS CONTINUE, BUT THIS TIME THE VICTIMS WERE NOT AS FORTUNATE AS I

-Citizens of Denver and the great state of Colorado, I plead for your help to find Elizabeth Sanders. She was abducted by the same three Colombian thugs who only a few days earlier attempted my abduction. Mrs. Sanders' husband James was brutally murdered during this horrific event.—Carolina Paige

Carolina's article was concise and to the point. She listed the facts and similarities between her abduction and Elizabeth's, but was careful not to alert or suggest to the reader that these crimes were connected to the Denver Mayor, or that there was some deeper criminal element behind this. She wrote nothing about her phone conversation with Diego. She also was careful not to incite wide-spread panic, by insisting that these two incidences were not random acts, but instead targeted and deliberate. At this time she did not want to speculate or offer conjectures without solid evidence, but assured her readers that both the *Post* and the FBI is investigating both cases as one. She stated that their main focus at that point was the safe return of Mrs. Sanders. Carolina was able to get a quote from Mayor Higgins' office, expressing shock and concern, not the Mayor himself but his secretary on acting on his behalf. Carolina concluded her article with the same request as Inspector Miller asked of her, she asked her readers "for prayers!"

Alongside Carolina's front page story were police artist sketches taken from descriptions provided by Carolina of the Colombian assailants. Other related articles written by other journalists were presented on the second and third pages. They mostly covered the Sanders, their careers with the city of Denver, and Elizabeth's role with the Denver Coalition.

Bruce was able to catch up on his sleep in an empty office while Carolina and Whitten and the crew at the *Post* worked diligently through the night. The Denver Police had posted uniformed guards at the main entrance and on their floor allowing Bruce to sleep easier.

As the sun peered over the eastern horizon, Bruce and Carolina exited the parking garage to head back to Kaleidospokes. In Bruce's rear view mirror he could see the assigned police cruiser which would accompany them for the immediate future.

Bruce delivered Carolina to her apartment and after he was convinced it was secure he went downstairs, briefly checked in with his Denver police counterparts, then joined Karl and his bicycle mechanic brigade inside. After greeting Bruce, they escorted him to the tiny back room, where he set up his surveillance command post. He had honored Carolina's request of no cameras inside her apartment, but did set a few around the perimeter with two focused on the front door. He also made sure that her GPS tracking device was working correctly, despite her staying at home. Bruce honored Carolina's request for no video cameras within her apartment, but she wasn't specific about audio listening devices, so he did run some wires up the old laundry chute.

Upstairs after brushing her teeth, Carolina went directly to her bed, bypassing her normal pre-sleep routine of returning emails and responding to messages on Facebook. Sleep came fast and it was continuous. She was very grateful that her slumber was uninterrupted. It was a rare few hours of peaceful dreamless bliss for her. She was so appreciative of this that she actually thanked Rebecca aloud."

CHAPTER 31

C arolina looked at her phone to see that it was 3:30 p.m. She alerted both Whitten and Bruce with a text announcing that she was awake and to give her thirty or forty minutes. Then she'd be ready to head back to the paper. She also inquired if either had heard anything and for which their response was "no"! After dropping a cup of French Roast in her Keurig, she started her shower, staying true to her normal a.m. routine, despite this altered late afternoon schedule.

Carolina left her phone on the night table beside her bed while she showered so she didn't hear her text alarm sound. Not until the eye liner stage of her routine did she realize that her phone was not on the vanity. So she peered around the corner into her bedroom to see a flashing screen coming from the nightstand. She scurried over to retrieve it. It was a text, but strangely there was no number or name indicating who sent it, and the message was bizarre as well: *"Gun Creek Lane, Steamboat."*

Carolina finished getting ready, then headed downstairs to collect Bruce for their jaunt back to the *Post*. A few minutes into the trip she reached into her purse and pulled out her phone, and stared at the mysterious text.

"So Bruce, do you know if it's possible to send a text on your phone and make it anonymous?"

Bruce turned his focus momentarily off the road to glance at Carolina, who was still staring at her screen.

"I suppose it's possible. Why?"

"I received a strange text with no number attached. It looks like an address."

"That's another new phone, isn't it? No one but our inner circle should have your number."

Carolina responded, "Yep!"

"We'll see what our FBI friends can make of it. I'll call Miller from my phone. I'm sure that he'll meet us at the *Post*." Bruce's conversation to Miller took less than ten seconds.

"He's sending Gonzales to meet us at the paper."

Carolina went directly to her office and turned on her laptop, with the intention of emailing her mom and sister. She wanted to alert them of her phone issues, but first she wanted to Google the text message she received to see what popped up, but when she pulled her phone from her purse the message was gone.

"Crap!" she thought, "Gun something, Steamboat, I should have written it down!" Carolina was furious with herself. She finished her emails just as Bruce stuck his head in the door.

"Gonzales is up with Whitten, he wants to see your phone."

"Great, but there's not much to see, the message is not there anymore. It just vanished." Carolina handed him the phone.

"Okay, let's go."

Carolina glanced back at her open laptop then fell in behind Bruce following him to the elevator. They exited on Whitten's floor and marched directly to the conference room, where they were greeted by agent Gonzales.

"Agent Miller was detained and your boss Mr. Whitten had to leave to take care of another issue, but he told me to tell you to stop by his office when we've concluded."

"Any news?" Carolina asked.

"Not yet, ma'am." Gonzales replied. "I understand you received an anonymous text."

Bruce handed Gonzales the phone.

"As mysteriously as it appeared, it has now disappeared." Carolina took the phone out of Gonzales's hand and opened it to her phone texts. "Still gone!" She handed the phone back. "As you can see, my new *Post* issued phone only has three texts, two from Whitten and one from Bruce. Inspector Miller, the IT guy who issued me the phone, Whitten and Bruce are the only ones who have my number."

"So what did the text say?" Asked Gonzales.

"Gun something, Steamboat. That's it."

Gonzales inspected the phone. He turned it off the restarted it. Carolina gave him her password and he opened the phone, but still could find no evidence of the text.

"Okay, I'm going to take this back to our lab.

"One more thing, in regards to the overall investigation, Inspector Miller wanted me to inform you that our handwriting experts did confirm that the letter you received from Bogotá was indeed written by Luis Vargas. The lab also discovered that the mysterious border around the letter had encrypted data inscribed in it."

"Encrypted data?" Carolina asked.

"Yes, apparently it had the name of a bank in Grand Cayman Island along with account and routing numbers.

Actually, that's why Miller could not make today's meeting. He's in the middle of contacting the bank, authorities on the island, our State Department and preparing a couple of agents to go to Grand Cayman.

"That's all the info we have now. When Inspector Miller has more he'll contact you. We'll be in touch!"

With that, their meeting concluded and Gonzales exited.

"Well Bruce, it looks like I need another phone. I can't wait to tell Whitten."

She and Bruce walked out of the conference room and down the hall to Whitten's office. His office door was closed. She knocked and peered through the glass partition adjacent his door. Whitten was on his phone, but looked up when he heard the knock and motioned them to enter. Carolina walked over to his desk and took a seat across from him while Bruce sat in a chair in an area off to the side. Whitten's phone conversation concluded in a few minutes, but he took another few minutes jotting down notes before acknowledging his newly-arrived guests.

"That was my Colombian private investigator. It seems one Diego Morales has come up missing. He just vanished, leaving behind no letters, explanations, nothing. There wasn't any sign of foul play. It did appear that some of his personal possessions, cell phone, toothbrush, razor and some clothes were gone, which normally indicates he left on his own accord."

"He also reported back on my request to find out where Mayor Higgins was spending his time and money when he visited Bogotá over the years. It seemed he always stayed at the Hilton and regularly ate at the same cafes, nothing out of sorts. They did uncover records dating back ten years."

"So what did I miss from your meeting with Agent Gonzales?"

Per Whitten's request, Carolina filled him in on their meeting including passing along their discovery of the inscribed bank information on Vargas's stationery. Whitten commented sarcastically at the FBI's collection of her cell phones, but subsequently ordered her another IPhone during their meeting.

Following their brief chat, she and Bruce headed back to her office. When they arrived Bruce took his position on the chair outside of her office, while she went in and sat down at her desk.

"What the heck!" Weren't exactly the words that raced through her mind when she read what was waiting for her on her laptop screen. There it was again, "Gunn Creek Lane, Steamboat."

"It's a damn address!" Carolina shouted. She quickly typed the sentence into Google Maps the sentence to confirm her suspicion and was in turn given back a vivid view of a street, Gunn Creek Lane, Steamboat Springs Colorado.

"What if," she thought, "an old gold mining town, now a skiing destination about seventy miles northwest of here is the hideout?"

She summoned Bruce. At the same time she picked up her land line phone and dialed Inspector Miller. As Bruce entered her office Miller answered his phone.

"Inspector," Her voice was frantic.

"Yes, Carolina. What's up?"

"I know this sounds completely absurd, but that text showed up again, this time on my laptop. But that doesn't matter. It's a street, Inspector! Gunn Creek Lane is a street in Steamboat Springs."

"Don't ask me how I know, but I just do. Elizabeth is somewhere on that street. Unless you have a more concrete idea as to where she's at, you need to start your search there. IMMEDIATELY!" She exuberantly declared.

"Hello, are you there?" cried out Carolina, as there was dead silence on the phone.

"Yes, I'm still here. You want me to dedicate men to a street in a ski resort town with nothing more to go on than an unexplained text on your phone? The reason my phone was silent, was because I was still trying to process that in my mind."

"Listen I'm sorry, you're right I do have nothing else concrete to go on. As soon as we hang up, I'll have someone start investigating Gunn Creek Lane. I apologize for snapping at you."

"Per my watch we only have two hours left before they kill Elizabeth and you are content just to start an agent investigating it." Carolina slammed the receiver down then looked at Bruce who had overheard the conversation.

CHAPTER 32

"Bruce, I'm going to Steamboat Springs, with or without you!" Carolina didn't look up. She was scrutinizing her laptop screen for the address, which just like on her phone, was now gone too.

"THERE'S NO WAY YOU'RE GOING WITHOUT ME!" declared Bruce.

"Neither one of you are going without me," came a voice from behind Bruce. It was Whitten standing in the doorway. He was delivering her new phone and heard most of the conversation to.

"Well what are you two waiting for? Let's roll!" Whitten ordered.

"I hope that you have more firepower?" Whitten asked.

Bruce responded, "Are you kidding me, I have an arsenal in my trunk! The hell with the FBI. We are going to Steamboat Springs to rescue Mrs. Sanders with or without their help!" Bruce followed Carolina and Whitten out the door and to the parking lot where they jumped into Bruce's car. Within minutes they were on U.S. 40 heading for Steamboat.

"Okay, Ms. Paige, it's blind faith that has us heading to a street in Steamboat. Other than this unexplained message showing up on your phone and laptop can you give me any more justification for this wild goose chase?" commented Whitten.

"No. Nothing that won't make you think that I'm insane," Carolina responded while gazing out the window."

"That's not exactly the answer that boosts my confidence. Bruce, I'm hoping that you have some sort of a plan once we get there. Like what happens if we do find Elizabeth?" Whitten asked.

"Well Sir, I've punched in Gunn Creek Lane and it shows we are one hour and forty five minutes away and we have only two hours before they said they would kill Mrs. Sanders, so my plan is not to be late."

It was a very stressful trip to Steamboat Springs, Whitten was lamenting the fact that that the *Post's* helicopter was on assignment at a Broncos preseason game. When they arrived at Gunn Creek Lane there were only a few chalets on the winding mountain road, but they didn't have enough time to check out each one.

Bruce pulled over and stopped, got out and went around the back to retrieve a shotgun and a 9mm Glock from the trunk. When he shut the lid, both Whitten and Carolina were standing next to him. They studied the satellite view of the houses on Google Earth trying to decide which residence looked to be the most potential.

"Carolina, you told me you used to go quail hunting with your family, I would suggest the light weight handgun unless you feel more at home with…"

Before he could finish, she grabbed the shotgun from Bruce and advanced a shell into to the chamber. Whitten took the Glock.

"These guns are only for your own self protection. From here on out, I work alone! I'll start going from house to house, you two hang back. Once we find the right house, I want one of you to call 911 and the other to call Inspector Miller. So, which drive do we start first, Whitten?"

Suddenly three Black Escalades flew around the corner. They slowed momentarily going around them. The last one rolled down its tinted window so that they could see it was Inspector Miller in the passenger seat.

"It looks like the Cavalry just arrived!" Yelled Bruce. "Come on, back in the car!"

They jumped in the car and followed the urgent procession about a mile to a narrow paved drive. The drive seemed to disappear up the grade and through the heavy woods, making the house invisible from the street. Bruce didn't follow them up the drive, but stopped at the entrance and they all got out. Carolina left behind the shotgun but reached in her bag and pulled out one of the tools of her trade, a camera.

"I'm going up!" She shouted.

"Not yet!" Bruce grabbed her arm. Just then they heard the humming of a helicopter above the tree-tops and three sedans pulled behind them. These cruisers belonged to the Colorado State Police.

Suddenly the unmistakable clapping sound of automatic gunfire erupted from the direction of the dwelling. The heavily armored policemen stormed by them with their automatic rifles.

Minutes seem like an eternity. The sound of gunfire soon ceased accentuating the only foreign sound left, which was the hum of the helicopter from above.

Bruce stood at attention, staring up the drive, his handgun tightly gripped at his side. Carolina and Whitten paced back and forth behind him.

Bruce turned and looked at Carolina. "Okay, stay close to me!"

They stared to walk, but the walk turned into jog. The grade was steep, so within five hundred yards, Whitten had to stop for wind, but Carolina and Bruce trudged on. They nearly went a half of a mile before they came to the opening in the woods and were able to view a stately chalet.

The grounds were teeming with vehicles, state police officers and FBI agents. Carolina began snapping photos of the scene. By the relaxed demeanor of the officers, it was apparent that the threat was over. But there was no eased demeanor for Carolina. The look of worry and fear was evident in her face. She ran to the nearest group of cops to ask the status of the hostage, but their answers were aloof and general. She scanned the crowd for Miller or Gonzales but didn't see them so she headed for the front door.

Just then Miller appeared in the doorway with his arm securely around Elizabeth. Carolina shrieked in jubilation, then looked to the sky to proclaim, praise be to God and she made the sign of the cross across her chest. She rushed over and threw her arms around both Inspector Miller and Elizabeth.

An ambulance rolled up and parked within in ten feet of where they embraced. The inspector and Carolina presented the very weak and dazed Mrs. Sanders to the paramedics.

Whitten finally made it up the drive and walked over to join them.

"I thought you weren't coming." Whitten directed his query to the Inspector and Carolina chimed in, "Yes, I believe your response was that you were 'passing it off to an agent' in other words, patronizing me."

"I did exactly that, I passed along this 'Gunn Creek Lane' text to an agent assigned to this investigation. It just so happens that this particular agent immediately recognized this street from data he obtained the day before while collecting asset information on Denver Mayor Higgins. Seems, the owner of this particular chalet is your mayor, Arthur Higgins. Too much of a coincidence. And, as you so intuitively alluded, we had nothing else. We obtained a search warrant and as it turns out God answered our prayers!"

"What about the assailants?" Asked Whitten.

"Deceased! Cause of death, government-issued lead. I'm sure that we will have to answer to our State Department for this, but I'm not going to jeopardize the safety of my men or the victim so that some politian can feel good about the treatment of our Colombian guests.

"We actually would have preferred to take at least one into custody so that we could obtain more information, but they were given that opportunity and chose to decline."

Carolina spoke up. "What about Diego, was he in there?"

"Agents are inside collecting data, including DNA samples and facial photos, but it doesn't appear that Senor Morales was part of this group."

CHAPTER 33

"*ELIZABETH SANDERS FREED FROM HER CAPTORS*"

The next morning's headline of the *Denver Post*. The subtitle written by Carolina Paige, ***Mrs. Sanders was found by the FBI and State Police in a ski chalet in Steamboat Springs, owned by Denver's Mayor, Arthur Higgins.***

Once again Carolina, Whitten and a team of writers worked diligently through the night to publish this front-page story. The meat of the story covered the fact that the Colombian abductors refused to surrender and were killed at the scene. She also wrote that the reasons for this abduction as well as her attempted abduction, plus her husbands' homicide are still unknown and that the FBI is continuing to investigate. Furthermore and in conclusion of her article, she pared the words 'suspicious oddity' to describe the fact that Sanders was an employee of the Mayor's office and was held hostage in the ski chalet which was owned by the mayor himself. Carolina's last sentence affirmed that "many questions still remained unanswered and several mysteries are in need of solving!"

Days passed with relatively no news in regard to this case. As expected the cities of Denver and Steamboat Springs were abuzz with rumors. This event was all anyone could talk about throughout Colorado; even the national news chains covered this story continuously.

The day after this event a distraught-looking Mayor Higgins gave a quick and prepared speech praising the FBI for saving the life of Elizabeth Sanders. He also said that he and his office would completely cooperate with their investigation. When he was done he took no questions despite a salvo from journalists in attendance.

Carolina checked with Inspector Miller daily but he was relatively tight-lipped, sighting several tentacles and very complex. He did confirm that Diego was not one of the bodies at the chalet. He promised once his team concluded their extensive investigation she would be the first and only journalist he would call.

Carolina was able to relax for the time being. She had no further calls from Diego and Rebecca let her sleep.

Finally, three weeks after the FBI raid on Mayor Higgins' chalet, warrants went out for his arrest. As promised by Inspector Miller, Carolina received a six a.m. call waking her. He informed her of Higgins' pending arrest on multiple charges of conspiracy, fraud, embezzlement and human trafficking as well as a party to extortion. Miller said the investigation was not over yet, but there was more than enough factual information to initiate Higgins' arrest. He expected the mayor to turn himself in and cooperate fully. Miller said that Colombia was also cooperating fully and they were in the process of searching for Diego Morales to take him into custody.

He warned her that in spite of her ordeal Denver Police were also considering bringing charges of conspiracy and theft of public funds against Elizabeth Sanders for her early involvement. If convicted, he doubted that she'd have to serve any time, just probation with public service.

Miller told her he needed to conclude their conversation, but invited her to come by his office later for more details.

Carolina woke Bruce up and jumped into the shower. Within minutes she was out the door and they were heading to the *Post*. She knew that Whitten wouldn't be there yet-so she called him on his cell phone and gave him the news.

With the information Inspector Miller provided, she was able to write a "Breaking News" bulletin for their webpage. After Whitten blessed it, and it was digitally posted, she went to her appointment with the FBI Inspector at his office.

Bruce drove Carolina to Miller's office. This trip would be his last assignment as his duties as full-time body guard and chauffer would be phased out. After seeking the advice of Inspector Miller a couple of days prior, Whitten, Carolina and Big Bruce mutually decided that she was not at risk anymore.

Miller was ready for her arrival, he had printed a copy of detailed evidence used for the FBI's briefing to the circuit court judge when they requested a search warrant of the Denver mayor's residence as well as his office.

"Here's what we've been able to piece together so far. It seems your Colombian friend Diego Morales, the mayor of Bogotá, Luis Vargas and Denver's Mayor Higgins were involved in a smuggling ring and they were using the Denver Homeless Coalition non-profit organization as their mode of operation. There were several facets of this criminal organization but the main object seemed to be the collection of cash. We were able to confirm what you already ascertained from Diego's own admission on your brief Limo ride. They were indeed funneling cash and monthly credit donations to a bank account set-up in the name Fuerzas Armadas in the Cayman Island."

"But they were also doing something even more sinister. They were involved in identity theft and human trafficking of the homeless and impoverished citizens here in Denver. In some cases, they sold their Social Security numbers, but we speculate that others were transported to Colombia and trained as mules to transport drugs or other illegal contraband back into the United States. Most of the Social Security numbers were auctioned to the highest bidder. Our foreign sources tell us that the Islamic state, known as ISIS is offering huge amounts of money for just one Social Security number. Strangely, we found significant monthly withdraws of cash from Mayor Higgins' account, but no deposits and we also found no numeric information regarding that Cayman account. If this were an equal crime ring, where is his cut? It appears he was working this end of the deal for free! We hope that he cooperates and can clear this up for us. The Cayman account also has monthly deposits of very large sums of money and bank notes from a Bogotá Bank, and the name on the account is Luis Francisco Vargas. He also has made no withdraws. There has been only one withdrawer from that Cayman account. It is Fuerzas Armadas and we believe that's an alias for Diego Morales."

"How is Senor Morales getting both Mayors to contribute their time and cash for no rewards?

"Blackmail!" Carolina blurted out.

Miller nodded. "That's what we speculate too. Blackmail. I'm guessing that it has something to do with Rebecca Wilson."

"The agency is investigating past relationships or acquaintances that the Mayor may have had with a Rebecca Wilson, but as of yet, no leads."

"By the way and not to sound condescending, but you do realize that the most or all of money in this account belongs to the Homeless Coalition, and cannot be given to the next of kin of this Rebecca Wilson."

Carolina realized that Inspector Miller knew nothing about Karl's relationship with Rebecca, but she said nothing. And of course Carolina had not shared with the Inspector or anyone except Karl her recent encounters with Becky.

She knew she needed to talk with Karl regarding his account of Becky's death. She also needed to convince him to talk to Inspector Miller, as she knew there was a strong chance that his Rebecca was also the same as

Luis Vargas' Rebecca, especially when you factor in that Vargas was staying in Denver around the same time Karl's Rebecca lost her life. Karl's information could prove to be very pertinent to the closure of this case.

Carolina also recognized that she was mentally exhausted and needed some time away from this drama, so when she returned to the *Post* she asked Whitten for some time off to visit her family in Indiana. Whitten was more than happy to grant her a well-deserved vacation; in fact he authorized the *Post* pay for her ticket to Indianapolis.

Carolina was so excited that she booked the next flight to Indy and called her mom with the good news. She doled out her goodbyes and hugs, then headed to the exit.

There was one final assignment she needed to do before grabbing her stuff and heading to the airport. She needed to have her chat with Karl.

Carolina's flight was scheduled to leave in a little less than two hours, so she ran up to her room and quickly packed enough for a week. After she crammed in her hair dryer, makeup and called a cab she was down to an hour and a half. "Plenty of time for a quick chat with Karl," she thought, that is if Karl were around.

When Carolina walked into Kaleidospokes she was informed that Karl was at the bank. So she visited with the boys until her cab arrived, but before she left instructed them to inform him that she was sorry she missed him and that she was returning to Indiana to visit with family and friends and hopefully, just rest.

"Also, tell your boss that Big Bruce will be by to collect his stuff, including this GPS broach that I've been wearing for over a month. Can you see that he gets this?" She handed one of the mechanics an envelope containing the GPS necklace.

"Bruce will also remove all of the wires from the laundry chute. I know you guys take turns at listening in!" Carolina playfully laughed seeing all the mechanics' faces turn red.

"I do want to talk with him first thing when I return," She shouted back as she exited through the door.

CHAPTER 34

Carolina had an enjoyable week back in the Hoosier state. She checked with Whitten and read the *Post's* webpage daily. It was hard for her to totally remove the recent events from thought when that was all her family and friends wanted to discuss. Only when she was sharing wine with her friends did she feel comfortable opening up.

It had been some time since she had a visit from Rebecca, and she was feeling a deep desire to talk to someone other than Karl about her. Her talk with Karl had proved to be therapeutic, she didn't feel the anxiety that she felt prior to speaking with him. There was relief in knowing that she wasn't going insane, a thought that did enter her mind earlier in the investigation.

"Today would be the day" she thought as she woke from her slumber one morning. Carolina knew that her mother was an early riser and that she would have her to herself for an hour or so. This would be an ideal time to chat over coffee.

"Good morning, Mom." As predicted Carolina's mom was up and milling around the kitchen, practically at the same time the sun was rising from the east. She wasn't expecting company, but was delighted to see her daughter. Immediately she grabbed another coffee cup from the cupboard and poured Carolina some coffee, and then she handed it to her and kissed her on her forehead.

"Mom, I need to talk to you." Immediately a concerned look came over her mom and Carolina picked up on it.

"I'm okay," she assured her. "I just need to open up about something and you're the only one I can comfortably trust to discuss this with. Plus, I just miss our little mom-daughter chats."

Immediately, her mother's worried look changed to a warm glow. She put her arm around Carolina and they walked to the kitchen table and sat.

Carolina had been researching ghost or spirit phenomenon on the web. She had also been reading her bible searching for answers. As always, the bible made her feel better, but she found nothing that satisfied her query as to why Rebecca's spirit was reaching out to her. She knew that her mom wouldn't have the answers either, but her mom would understand.

So, Carolina started talking, and her mother listened intently. She started at the beginning and explained that shortly after she moved into her tiny apartment over the bicycle shop she began having terrifying nightmares. She vividly and with detail told her mom of the surreal dreams, of reliving the visions through the eyes of this child. Every night and each dream revealed the progression of this child into a young woman, and this young woman was always accompanied by her bicycle.

Carolina told her mom of Karl's relationship with a woman called Rebecca and how she lived in Carolina's apartment until her tragic death in 1967. She told her of the chill she got after learning that her bike was hanging right below her bed. She told her mom of her encounters with this cyclist in Bogotá and how the female cyclist left her subconscious and took on a physical presence that watched over her. Carolina even told her mother how the mayor of Bogotá seemed to have a haunting relationship of sorts with this cyclist and that he mistook her for this Rebecca. She told of his deep-seated hatred evolving from a past relationship with the Mayor of Denver, possibly over this cyclist named Rebecca.

Carolina's story went full circle back to Denver, as she summarized the mysterious parallels of three men, a female cyclist, a revolutionary Colombian crime syndicate, and of course, most recently a young journalist.

Carolina's mother sat mesmerized for more than an hour listening to her daughter pour out every little detail of her saga.

"So Mom, now that you've heard my entire sordid account, do you think your daughter is crazy?"

"Oh my goodness dear! I just need a moment to soak this all up." She took a large gulp of her now cold coffee and then continued.

"First of all, I don't think you're crazy, actually I believe that you're blessed! God must have connected you to this Angelic spirit, for some intended purpose. And, that purpose may never be revealed to you here on earth. So just accept it and have faith."

"What do you think, Carolina? Did this spirit need your help to dismantle this Colombian-Denver crime syndicate, or is there something more? You say you've not had any encounters or dreams in quite some time."

Carolina shrugged her shoulders, "I honestly don't know."

"Would you like to drive up to South Bend and talk with one of your old professors at Notre Dame?" Carolina's mother reached out across the table and took hold of her hands.

"Mom, our little talk this morning did me more good than listening to the pompous opinions of any professor. I was looking for some profound incite as to why I was chosen by this female apparition to be her medium of sorts and as always you provided just that. You comforted me when you said, 'God must have connected me to assist Rebecca', so I say, in God's hands my faith will lie."

"Thank you, dear," Mrs. Paige smiled with a loving gaze back at her daughter, but then immediately drifted into deep thought, as if she suddenly was deeply bothered.

"Rebecca? You say her name is Rebecca? Do you know her last name?"

"Yes, it's Wilson, Rebecca Wilson."

Mrs. Paige's face turned white as a sheet.

"Good morning ladies. What did I miss?" Carolina's father entered the room. Carolina jumped up and gave her father a kiss, but her mother sat stoic, still deep in thought and said nothing.

"Mom, are you alright?" She didn't respond to Carolina, instead looked directly at her husband and asked.

"Paul, didn't you have a cousin who was killed in Denver sometime back in the sixties?"

Mr. Paige looked at his wife a bit bewildered and Carolina gave her a glare as if she was just betrayed, as she was not quite ready to share this secret with her father.

"Ah, yes, actually she was my second cousin, Cousin Becky, Rebecca Wilson. She was hit and killed by a car while riding her bike. I was just seven years old, but I still vividly remember my mother crying uncontrollably, when she got the phone call. Carolina, I can't believe that I never have told you about your cousin Becky, she was one remarkable lady!"

Mr. Paige suddenly realized that his audience was a little too captive. As he was now looking at the attentive faces of his wife and daughter, looking stunned to what they just heard.

"What's wrong? Why did you ask me about Cousin Becky?" Mr. Paige sheepishly asked.

"Dad, go grab a cup of coffee. You are going to need to sit down!"

The feelings of comfort that Carolina received earlier from her mother were now gone after hearing the unfathomable news that she may actually be related to

Rebecca. Immediately she craved more information about Rebecca.

Before Carolina opened up to her father, she asked him to tell her more of what he remembered about their Cousin Becky, which of course he obliged.

"It's been a long time, but he would do his best. Becky's mother died shortly after she was born and her father was institutionalized a few years later. By-the-way, Becky's father was your great grandfather's brother. Apparently the Colorado authorities had difficulty getting in touch with my grandparents or her aunt, so the state took her as well."

"I recall a conversation at the dinner table several years later, of how terrifying it must have been for Becky, just a toddler, to endure the dreadful conditions of the sanitarium, until her Aunt Beth and my grandfather could retrieve her. So very sad!"

He paused for a moment, and then his face lit up.

"After all of her tribulations as a child, Becky found refuge in of all things a bicycle. She was the first female to peddle her bike from coast to coast consecutively, an amazing feat for anyone, especially a female in 1967."

Carolina recalled in her mind that her dad's account was very similar to the version which Karl told her.

When her dad said that it was all that he could recall about Rebecca, Carolina, with encouragement from her mother, proceeded to divulge her saga as she did a little over an hour ago to her mom.

"So, Dad one of the first nights after I moved into my little apartment over the bicycle shop, I had a nightmare about a little girl. She was locked in a tiny room resembling a prison cell. She was terrorized and even strangled until a nun pulled her from the clutches of a faceless evil. Until now I didn't know what this place was or more importantly who this little girl was."

"Dad, I have a lot of unbelievable events to tell you. I know this will be hard to digest, because right now I'm having trouble with it too. I just hope, that like Mom, you'll believe me when I'm done. More importantly, I hope that you won't think that I need to be institutionalized too." Carolina smiled awkwardly.

Her Dad wasn't as receptive as her mother and didn't have a lot to say when she was done. Never-the-less he gave her a hug and kiss, but the subject wasn't discussed for the rest of her visit.

CHAPTER 35

C arolina's week went fast, but by the end she was ready to get back to her apartment in the 'mile high city' and back to work at the *Post*.

It was late when she arrived and Kaleidospokes was closed, so her greetings to Karl and the boys would have to wait until morning. After lugging her travel bag up the exterior staircase and hoisting it on her bed she noticed a note from Bruce wishing her a good night sleep without all the wires.

Carolina woke early. She was excited to see her buddies' down-stairs, especially Karl. She couldn't wait to inform him of the news that she was related to his Rebecca.

When she went downstairs she was surprised to see that they were all waiting and greeted her with roaring cheers as she walked through the door. Karl, smiling from ear to ear, handed her a cup of coffee which she took, then set it down to give him a jovial hug. Of course as not to leave out anyone, she individually doled out hugs to all the mechanics.

Karl ordered them back to work and Carolina and he retreated to the kitchen where they would end up chatting for hours.

Because of his empathetic response to her prior confessional conversation about Rebecca, telling Karl about the bizarre possibility of being a distant cousin came a little easier.

At first Karl thought she was jesting, but after realizing that she was not, he became skeptical and even a little defensive. However the more they talked and the more she divulged, such as that Rebecca was raised by her aunt and that she had relatives who lived in Indiana, facts that Karl had not revealed to her yet, he warmed up to the notion that maybe Carolina could indeed be blood related.

After mulling over the exhausting possibilities of karma, fate or even revenge, Carolina changed their conversation and asked him to tell her of the events as best he could remember of the night Rebecca was killed. Karl's eyes misted as he told her that it was the worst day in his life. He admitted that he was devastated. His world came crashing down that day and he has never been the same since.

"It was a late night and we were at a get-together at a friend's house. Actually Becky met me there after one of her long training rides. Becky didn't drink and always felt awkward around my friends whenever we got together. Well by the time she arrived, I was already on my third glass of wine. She quietly requested that I slow down a bit and that's when tensions flared. She wanted to go, I didn't and told her I was staying. A spat occurred and she left. The night was foggy and cold. I sent Rebecca to her death!" Karl started sobbing.

Carolina gave him a few moments then responded. "Karl, you have to let this go!" He didn't reply and she had no further comment, so she changed the subject. "What about the driver?" Karl shook his head. "The son of a bitch didn't even stop! The cops gave up their investigation after only a week. The driver or the vehicle was never found. I swore that I would track down and kill this animal who struck down my Becky! I even saved up money to hire a private investigator but they too came up with nothing. Many years have passed and I guess the revenge within me has faded, but the guilt still burns as hot as it did the day after!"

They sat saying nothing for several minutes. Carolina searched for something to say, then finally she spoke.

"You were damn lucky that you were not able to perform your revenge killing. That only would have resulted in your incarceration. Your gilt would be doubled and she would have been still, just as dead. Perhaps you were spared from making this foolhardy mistake. Perhaps you can still assist the FBI in helping find out who killed Becky. Who knows? Maybe she's come back to help you through me. Karl, I believe that all of the events which have happened recently are somehow connected."

"Both, Luis Vargas and Diego mentioned Becky and the FBI knows this. They don't know, nor would they believe that she also saved my life and led me to find Elizabeth Sanders. Karl I think you should talk with Inspector Miller and tell him what you just told me. Maybe nothing will come of it, but maybe something will. Maybe you hold the last piece of the puzzle that will solve this mystery."

Karl thought a moment then responded, "You must be related to my Becky for you are just as wise as she!"

CHAPTER 36

Carolina was able to convince Karl to talk with Inspector Miller, and Carolina talked the Inspector into giving her permission to interview Mayor Arthur Higgins who was released from jail, but under house arrest until his trial. The inspector was clear with her that she still needed to get his and his legal team's permission, but he would ask.

Carolina, asked him to inform the mayor that she only wanted to ask him one thing. It had to do with something that his former friend Luis Vargas had said to her in his final letter before he allegedly took his own life.

Carolina's plan worked. Higgins took the bait. He told Inspector Miller that she could talk with him, under the conditions of no camera or recording device and that she only had twenty minutes. Of course Carolina accepted and the next day she arranged for Miller to escort her onto the mayor's gated estate and up to the front door.

Instead of sending a surrogate, Miller decided to do this chore himself thinking Carolina might actually dig up something that could help his case.

The door was as far as he was allowed without Higgins' legal representation there, so the Inspector sat on the front steps and waited for Carolina. He learned later that Higgins on his own accord chose not to involve his attorneys for his conversation with Carolina.

Carolina was greeted at the door by a stocky middle aged man with greased back hair dressed in a tight suit. His appearance was intimidating enough that Inspector Miller stood up and unbuttoned his sport coat just in case he needed quick access to his federally issued equalizer holstered under his left arm. The man glanced at Miller then back at Carolina and growled, "You here to see the Mayor?"

"Yes I'm Caro…"

Before she could finish her name, he growled again, "Follow me!"

He turned and glared at Miller, giving him a look from top to bottom. "He stays here!"

Carolina followed him as instructed to the mayor's study where he was waiting behind a desk.

Glaring at her, the mayor spoke, "You've got twenty minutes starting now, so you'd better be concise and get to the point!"

"I will get right to the point and thank you for seeing me," Carolina began.

"I took a little trip to Bogotá Colombia to visit your acquaintance, Luis Vargas. After I returned home from the trip, Luis sent me a letter, and as it turned out, his final letter. In his poignant letter, Luis mentioned you and also a statement, which I am having trouble understanding. I was hoping that you could help. If I may?" She reached inside her purse and pulled out a copy of the letter, and showed it to him, so that he could see Vargas' signature.

Higgins sarcastically made a facial gesture, which didn't faze Carolina, as she continued, "So Mr. Mayor, what do you think Vargas meant when he said and I quote 'I've *allowed Arthur Higgins to control my life, my soul.*' Vargas makes several disparaging allegations against you, including calling you a '*horrible hombre.*' What can you tell me about this?"

Higgins face turned red with anger and it was obvious to Carolina that she had just struck a nerve, so she came right back with the kill question. "Also, there is the mystery of his final sentence, *he wanted the good people of Denver to know, that he was not driving*. Why do you think he felt so compelled to make this declaration in a letter which he intended as his closing avowal?"

"During Luis Vargas's stay at your home, was there some sort of incident or accident? Were you involved as well? Arthur Higgins, who was Rebecca?" Carolina amped up her volume.

"Listen, I know that the FBI has already asked you these questions, but I want you to know that I am not here as a journalist from the *Denver Post*. This is way more personal than that! I know who Rebecca was, and I know you and Luis Vargas ran her down and killed her." Higgins spun his chair around so that he was facing the opposite way.

"LOOK AT ME, YOU BASTARD! Why did you not stop?" Carolina just realized that she had stepped way over the line and let her emotions cloud her journalistic judgment. But, regardless the end result was quite effective.

With his back still turned Higgins requested to his body guard that he leave the room. After he heard the door shut he spun his chair around, and then stood up. The Mayor was obviously shaken and there were tears flowing from his eyes.

"Yes, I WAS DRIVING! I was driving because I was the least drunk of the two of us! ARE YOU HAPPY? We did stop, she was already gone, and there was nothing that we could do. I don't know, maybe we panicked. I had to pull Luis off of her, he was screaming. It was awful! I There's not a day that goes by, that I don't see that vision in my head."

"I don't know why I let Vargas extort me for all of those years! God have mercy on my soul!"

Carolina interrupted Higgins, "Wait a minute, what did you just say?"

"I was so worried about my political career that I let this vile piece of crap, not only extort me, but use me as a crime partner, stealing funds from the Homeless Coalition. One crime led to another and here I am now."

"What a joke, I would like to know, how I controlled his life and soul?"

Carolina walked over to him, stood toe to toe, and looked up into his eyes, "Are you saying you did not extort money from Luis Vargas, but in fact just the opposite? You were the one who was being extorted?"

Higgins shook his head, looking confused but answered emphatically, "Yes, that is what I am saying! And, your fifteen minutes is up!" Carolina didn't argue that the agreed time was for twenty minutes.

"Ms. Paige, if you have a chance to talk to any of Rebecca Wilson's family, tell them that I can never replace their loved one, and I don't expect to be forgiven, but let them know that I am truly remorseful for what I have done!"

Carolina acknowledged that she heard his request, turned around and started to walk toward the door, when the sound of a loud clap reverberated though the room and stopped her progression. A large book lay open on the floor. It appeared that it inexplicably fell from the bookcase which lined the wall. Carolina proceeded with her exit which took her in the direction of the book. She kneeled down and picked it up. It was the bible and it was opened to Luke 6:37.

Carolina remembered that chapter very well, as it was one of her Notre Dame Professor's favorite to recite. Carolina drew the book close and she began to read out loud. *"Do not judge and you will not be judged. Do not*

Condemn and you will not be condemned. Forgive, and you will be forgiven."

She walked over to the Mayor and handed it to him, still opened. "Maybe you've already been forgiven."

Carolina walked out of his office, marched to the front door, reconnected with Inspector Miller on the front step and they left the premises.

Even though his confession to Carolina probably wouldn't hold up in court, she told Miller everything just the same, including what he said regarding his version of who was extorting whom.

Weeks went by and the FBI's investigation continued. Carolina moved onto writing other articles, awaiting new developments or the trial, which was tentatively set for three months ahead. Higgins' defense team was appealing to get an extension with a new venue, arguing political bias.

For her efforts Carolina received a promotion with a new title of 'Lead Investigation Reporter' and more importantly a salary bump from the *Post*. She was quoted from her articles by other news print outlets and did numerous morning show interviews, both locally and nationally. Carolina was rapidly becoming a household name in Colorado. Her name was now being mentioned for nominations for prestigious journalism awards. As a result of her new found fame, Carolina was now receiving job offers from cable news networks, a lifelong dream of hers.

CHAPTER 37

I t was Friday at 5:35 p.m. Carolina headed home after a long week of work. Her plans for the evening included relaxing with a glass of wine, calling her mother to discuss occupational scenarios as a television correspondent and if she could revitalize herself, meeting some of her friends later at a club.

When she pulled to the curb in her normal parking spot, she noticed something a little out-of-sorts, especially for a Friday night at Kaleidospokes. Usually Karl sends the boys home at five, but he remains keeping the store open until eight. Tonight the store was dark and the closed sign was on the door. Carolina started walking in that direction to peek in the window, but shrugged it off instead and headed up the stairs to her apartment. While climbing the steps, a solemn thought crossed her mind.

That is she did accept that job offer and relocate to New York City, how she would miss Karl and his mechanics.

Reinforcing this thought was something waiting for her on her doormat, a dozen red roses with an attached typed note, requesting her immediate presence downstairs.

Carolina smiled and thought, "What have they done now?" She unlocked her door, walked in just long enough to toss her stuff on the bed, do a quick make-up and hair refresh and then she was back out the door. She reached down and picked up the vase of roses and headed down the steps.

A surprise party of sorts was not exactly what she was looking for this Friday night, however the Kaleidospokes gang were like family and she knew her time with them was fleeting, so she put on her happy face and with flowers in one hand she grabbed the door handle and went in to the store.

''They're really going all out," she thought, as the showroom was completely dark and silent.

"Hello! Karl! Anyone?"

As her eyes adjusted, she saw a light coming from the back kitchen area and she could see a trail of rose petals on the floor leading in that direction.

"Guys where are you?" Carolina yelled, playing along with their little game.

She slowly followed the trail of petals to the door of the kitchen continuing to speak so they could hear her progression.

"Okay," she thought to herself, "I hope that I don't pee my pants when they try and scare me when I open the door."

She reached out and knocked on the door. Then with the same hand grabbed the knob slowly turning and pushing it open. The room appeared to be empty at least from where she was standing at the doorway. She did hear something that sounded like a low muffled groan coming from inside, so she slowly stepped past the threshold.

To her horror, in the corner sat Karl, bound and gagged. His swollen face splotched black and red, showing signs of being severely bludgeoned. Carolina let out a blood-curdling scream and released the vase, sending the bouquet of roses plummeting to the floor. Karl's eyes were wide open and he was rocking his chair back and forth, desperately trying to tell her something. She started toward him, but his eyes shifted past her. He began nodding toward the door. Carolina started to turn around when she felt the intense sting of something penetrating her skin on the back of her neck. By impulse reaction her hands went immediately to the area of pain, but just as they reached their target a jolt of electricity hit her body knocking her to the floor. Carolina rolled in agony as another charge struck, paralyzing her and rending her unconscious.

CHAPTER 38

"Awake, my sleeping beauty," a familiar voice called summoning her back from unconsciousness.

Senses were beginning to be restored to Carolina as the blood returned to her brain. As she became more alert she began to feel the excruciating pain, the residual effects resulting from being shot by a stun gun. Suddenly she felt a splash of cold water hit her face.

"Wake up you wretch!" Her eyes flew open to see the ominous figure belonging to the voice.

"Diego," Carolina muttered.

"Ta-da! In the flesh!" Diego did a pirouette and then bowed. "Someone's not happy to see me!"

Carolina found herself, like Karl duct taped in a chair and positioned so that she was facing him a few feet away. Karl was still gagged but now appeared to be unconscious.

She noticed that off to the side of him and on the floor was a wooden club.

"Your old Greek amigo put up quite the fight," Diego smirked.

"You killed him!" Carolina screamed.

"Oh relax, he's not dead yet. You're going to finish him off, not me."

Carolina looked at Diego puzzled by his statement, but didn't reply.

Diego continued. "Before you kill him, Senorita, I want you to hear a little story. In fact maybe old bicycle man would like to hear this too. Diego picked up the glass he used to douse Carolina, refilled it with water and then poured it on top of Karl. Who immediately jerked his head back, as he woke abruptly. Karl's eyes were intense with fury, but he could do nothing but listen.

"Buenos, amigo, glad you could join us. I was about to tell Senorita Paige a story of how I was able to extract money from Senors Luis Vargas and Arthur Higgins and convince them both that the other one was responsible for the blackmail," Diego laughed to himself.

"You see many years ago when I was just a young boy my mother worked as an el sirviente for the Vargas family; my father, their grounds keeper. Unlike many of my childhood compadres, when I got old enough to hold a broom, I was inducted into working alongside my mother."

"My family lived on the Vargas estate, our quarters were next to the equestrian barn. Mother and Father would work sixteen long hours a day for this swine and for a pittance salary. Many mornings my father could not stand up straight after shoveling horse dung the day before, and my Mother often would faint from exhaustion and lack of nourishment."

"Many unpleasant memories! Many lashings! I actually was severely punished for breaking a vase which I witnessed Senor Luis knocking over. Lashed for the crime and again for lying about it!"

Diego was shaking with ferocity. Pacing back and forth across the room Diego began a montage of rants, not necessarily for the benefit of Karl and Carolina, but for himself.

"When Master Vargas was off to school, I would sneak into his room and look at his treasures. One day I came upon some letters that were written in English, I assumed from the United States. This was soon after his stay here in Denver with Senor Higgins' family.

I was very curious

"I was very curious and intrigued, but I was just learning to read Spanish, and had no comprehension of English. However I knew someone who did, an older cousin. When I knew that Senor Vargas would not be home for a few days, I took the letters. I also swiped a couple of silver cufflinks and bartered with my elder cousin to read me the letters in exchange for the cufflinks. I listened and I took very good notes, including the name Arthur Higgins and his address.

"Oh I found out much about Senor Luis' adventure in Denver Colorado U.S.A, including how he and Senor Higgins got themselves drunk one night and then running over and killing a young American girl on a bicycle.

"I returned the letters but never forgot the story."

"Years later after a stint in the Colombian Army and then the People's Army, or Fuerzas Armadas Revolucionarias de Colombia, I returned working for the Vargas Family. This time it was for Senor Luis."

"I started as his personal butler, and then was his liaison; finally what would be the equivalence of what you Americans call a 'Chief of Staff.'"

"Do you know what it's like working for someone whom you totally despise? *Of* course you don't! The *;inmanable! ;juemadre!*" Diego paused sharing his perspective crime saga to interject a derogatory question for which his captive audience didn't reply.

"Well, where was I? Oh yes. So, part of my duties was collecting his mail and one day there it was, another letter from Senor Higgins. I opened it and this time, several years later, I could read it myself. Higgins invited Senor Vargas to Denver to discuss Denver's Homeless Coalition and potential partnerships between Bogotá and Denver regarding this, but I had a better idea. I took some of Luis Vargas' stationery and typed a response. Not as myself, but acting as Senor Vargas. I wrote that I would not be able to attend per his request, but I did have a proposition that would involve his Homeless Coalition and my proposition he should not refuse. I told him that I expected monthly deposits of funds be made into an account that I would set up in exchange for not sharing to the citizens of Denver, Colorado my account of the night that he ran down, then left to die an American girl. I will tell them how I begged you to stop, but you laughed then threatened me never to tell anyone. I will explain every detail so the police will know that I am not lying. I told him that I expected not just funds from his personal bank account but also funds generated from his Homeless Coalition account. A few years later, I expanded my request to include identifications of homeless and even the use of the homeless citizens themselves. I think you refer to these people as 'mules'."

"So that was your Mayor Higgins, but why stop there? Luis Francisco Vargas would be an es una nota dupe! With some help from my computer, I was able to duplicate Higgins' stationery. Then I took the liberty to type out my own special letter to Vargas. This time I played the role of your Mayor Higgins. The story was a bit different but the request was the same."

"So within days money was flowing into my account and from both Mayors, and the beauty of this was that they both thought that the other one was the blackmailer. How genius am I, right?"

"Well, for years everything was working flawlessly. I was becoming a very rich Colombian and because I was also very generous with my donations to my beloved FARC I was also very well respected. But, then my amigo Luis Vargas goes and gets brain cancer and decides to confess his sins and confront what he believes to be his blackmailer Arthur Higgins. You got involved and the rest is all too unfortunate."

"I underestimated the cunningness of Vargas and didn't foresee his ability to freeze the account and change the routing numbers. Of course, I would never dream he would then send you the new account numbers."

"Here's where I take back control. You Senorita Paige will hand over those Cayman bank account numbers and you will kill your pathetic old friend."

Carolina angrily interjected. "You cannot make me kill Karl!"

"Oh yes I can." Diego walked over to a black duffel bag on the floor, picked it up then brought it to a nearby counter, where both Karl and she could see.

"My little black bag of tricks," Diego smirked. "Let me see." He reached in and pulled out a stun gun and set it aside, then a 9mm Glock inside a plastic bag and finally a black box.

"You realize that in order to be a really successful Colombian businessman, you must also be an excellent pharmacist too." He opened the box and pulled out a syringe.

"Remember your limousine ride with my associates? You were deprived of my little narcotic cocktail then, but not today! Oh, I changed the dosage a bit, to make you very agreeable to my demands. In a moment I will inject you with my serum. We will take a little walk upstairs, find those account numbers, return here and you will shoot

Senor Karl in the head. One more thing and this is very important, I must not forget, while you are committing your vile murderous act, I will be videoing everything on your phone! You see, Senor Karl here, found out too much of your blackmailing scandal and you had no other choice but to eliminate him."

Diego walked over and plunged the needle deep in the back of Carolina's neck. She screamed and Karl jerked his chair back and forth nearly tipping it over.

"Well we have a few seconds before the serum reacts so let me tell you our plan. The FBI knows me to be the mastermind behind this impressive escandalo, but they didn't know that I had a silent partner. And surprise, it's you! Don't worry, I will go over the details more thoroughly with you later and of course your secret identity will be safe with me, that is, if you are obedient and see to my wishes."

"You twisted little twit! I do not have the damn bank account information. Vargas encrypted it in a letter which is now in the possession of the FBI." Carolina interjected.

"You are either a liar or a very bad journalist! No journalist gives up a special document like that without copying it first. However, it doesn't matter. In a few minutes

I will ask you if you possess a copy of the encrypted letter and you will have no choice but to tell me the truth."

Within a few minutes Carolina was feeling the effects of his injection. At first she acted tipsy as if she was drunk, but then her persona changed to more of a zombie-like trance. Her eyes glassed over and became sunken, her face became pale. Moments earlier she was loud and chatty, now she was quiet and emotionless.

Diego bent over and looked into her impassive eyes. "Senorita Paige, are you with us? Do you hear my voice?"

"Yes." She murmured.

"My voice will be the only voice which you will obey!" Diego then raised his voice a few octaves. "Do you understand?"

"I understand." Carolina spoke softly and monotonic.

"I am going to untie you now, and you will obey my every command! Do you agree?"

"Yes!"

"I am going to ask you a question in a minute and you must answer me correctly." Diego took a pair of scissors and began cutting away the duct tape from her arms and legs.

"Do you possess the letter or a copy of the letter from Luis Vargas that contains the Cayman Island bank account information?"

Without hesitation, Carolina responded, "No!"

Diego became very angry, cursing a few words in Spanish, then he kicked Carolina's chair causing her to tumble onto the floor.

"Get up you ignorant bitch! Why did you not copy such an important letter?" Diego turned his back and walked a few paces away, while Carolina picked herself off the floor.

"Because I took a picture of the letter on my phone," Carolina responded.

Diego's face lit up with excitement, then repeated what she said, "You took a picture on your phone? And, I actually have your phone. How convenient!"

"No," Carolina mumbled.

"What do you mean, no?"

"The picture was taken on my old phone and backed-up to Icloud."

"I don't even know what you are talking about, but I am losing my patience!" Diego screamed.

"Okay, I'm recomposed. Forget about the damn bank account information. You will get that to me later, but now we must finish business, and then I will be leaving. I back to Colombia and you, up to your apartment with a bottle of tequila. You got so drunk after work that you didn't hear the gunshot. You also won't remember a thing. Diego reached again in his black bag and pulled out two pairs of rubber gloves. He instructed Carolina to put one pair on, while he put on the other pair. He then placed his hands on her shoulders and walked her over directly in from of Karl's chair. Finally, he reached into the plastic sack and pulled out the gun.

"Okay old man, this is going to sting a bit!" Karl was so weak at this point he could barely raise his head.

Diego advanced a bullet into the chamber and placed the gun in Carolina's hand, extending her arm toward Karl.

"Okay, hold steady, but don't pull the trigger until I tell you."

"Okay."

Diego walked to the table and grabbed Carolina's phone, pointed it and pushed the record button.

"When you hear me slap my hand on the table, shoot Karl in the head."

Carolina shook her head slowly from side to side as if to acknowledge, no, but responded verbally with "okay".

270

She was trying to fight the effects of the drug cocktail as it was beginning to wear off.

Diego did not want his voice recorded, so he opted to signal her instead. He raised his hand to slap the table, but hesitated when he heard a noise from out in the showroom. As he wheeled around to investigate, a bicycle streaked through the door and across the room striking Carolina in back of her legs, keeling her backward. As she collapsed to the floor the gun she gripped flew out landing near Diego's feet. Diego dropped Carolina's phone and immediately reached down picking up the weapon.

"Who's there?" He cried out. Diego instinctively grabbed Carolina pulling her up and placing the dark blue cylinder against her temple. He then pulled her over next to the door and shouted into the dark store. "I've got a gun pointed directly at Senorita Paige's skull. If you don't show yourself immediately I'm going to blow her brains all over her pretty little blouse!

While he focused his attention into the showroom, something just as mysterious as the sailing bike was happening behind him. The tape which was adhering Karl to the chair started unfurling and then dropped to the floor. Diego heard the chair move as Karl struggled, rising up. Diego pushed Carolina down, recoiled and shot in the direction of the sound. His bullet struck Karl in the chest, dropping him immediately. The bicycle which was erect and stationary, as if someone were holding it, at that moment fell over.

Diego swung back around but this time it was his turn to meet his fate. Another gun was fired and the intended target was Diego. The copper jacketed projectile hit the Colombian in the forehead, killing him before he hit the floor.

It was Big Bruce!

He immediately went over to Carolina and assisted her from the floor to a chair. Then he walked to Karl, knelt down and applied pressure on his neck, searching for a pulse, a pulse which didn't exist. Bruce then stood, grabbed a towel, wetted it and returned to Carolina to dab her forehead. She was beginning to come out of her trance and the wet towel helped advance the process. Suddenly, as if a switch were turned on, she snapped from her drug-induced state.

It took her a minute to comprehend where she was. Once she did, she was horrified and became hysterical. She did not remember the events which just took place, or why she was sitting in Kaleidospokes' kitchen with two bodies on the floor immersed in pools of blood. Carolina had absolutely no idea what led to this calamitous situation.

Minute-by-minute more of her faculties returned. Then it clicked that one of the bodies on the floor was her beloved Karl and she began screaming, "It's all my fault! I'm sorry! I'm so sorry!"

Bruce threw his arms around her and helped her to her feet, with the intent of getting her out of the room, but instead they froze in their tracks, as they were now witnessing the unexplainable.

Karl sat up! Then he stood up! As he rose his weathered features seemed to smooth out and his hair thickened and changed in shade. His stature suddenly changed too into a youthful physique of a man half his age. He stood for a moment as if to get his bearings, or perhaps to wait on someone to join him. Carolina and Bruce still paralyzed, said nothing, they just stared in awe. The sounds of approaching sirens were evident, but they didn't heed, as they were oblivious to anything else but the occurrence that they were witnessing.

Soon a mist formed beside Karl and the mist took shape, and then the shape turned into a being. Tears formed in Carolina's eyes, again, as the mist formed a familiar shape, and the being was Rebecca. She had her arm entwined around his and they were staring into each other's eyes. They took a step, and then a couple more. Then they reverted back to mist and vanished completely. However, just before they disappeared, Becky turned to Carolina, smiled and deliberately moved her lips slowly to gesture a "Thank you!"

On the floor behind their grand departure, remained the bloodied body of Karl Kaleido, but his spirit was now on the other side, escorted by his only true and undying life companion.

Carolina stopped grieving momentarily, and the overwhelming pain of the guilt she was experiencing subsided as a result of what she just witnessed. She even felt a bit of closure. Warm thoughts immediately flowed into her brain, like perhaps God allowed Rebecca to wait in purgatory until it was Karl's time, so that they could enter heaven together. Maybe God also allowed her to put an end to this deplorable crime saga, construed by an evil individual and at her expense.

Carolina turned and looked up at Bruce, as tough as he was, he was not reacting the same as she. His complexion was pale with fear and his hands were trembling. "What just happened?" Bruce asked.

"Are you okay?" Carolina asked.

"I'm not sure," he responded. A buzz went off in Bruce's pocket. "I better get this." Bruce took out his phone and responded to the incoming call.

"The premises is secure. Two bodys in the back kitchen. Ms. Paige and I are heading toward the front door." Then he stuck his phone back in his pocket, put his arm around Carolina and started walking toward the exit. Seconds later the building filled with body-armored police and FBI. Inspector Miller approached them first inquiring about their condition. They both responded with "we're okay."

Miller lingered a little longer staring at Bruce. "Are you sure, Watt? You look like you just saw a ghost," Carolina sheepishly smiled, but Bruce didn't respond. Miller was satisfied enough with their response and quickly moved to the grizzly scene in the kitchen.

Carolina and Bruce walked to the lounge area and sat down. Carolina compassionately put her hand on Bruce's shoulder and said. "So big Guy, in a few days we'll get together for a cup of coffee and I'll tell you all about Rebecca Wilson. Okay?"

Bruce turned and looked at Carolina. "Yeah, I'm going to need that talk. When we give our testimony to these guys, let's leave the part out where Rebecca and Karl's spirits walk off into the afterlife. Deal?"

"That's a deal!" Carolina squeezed his arm and Bruce looked back at the crime scene.

"I know that you said that you are okay, but the paramedics are outside. I think they should check you out. Between the jolt of electricity and the drug cocktail, it's wise to be safe."

Carolina nodded her head in agreement, so Bruce got up and started walking to the door to summon them, but Carolina stopped him with one more question. "So, Bruce, what made you decide to drop by Kaleidospokes tonight?"

He hesitated a second before responding.

"I got a text on my phone. It simply said, *You're needed urgently at the bicycle shop.*"

"From whom?" Carolina asked.

"It was unidentified, just like your text a few weeks ago, directing you to where Elizabeth was. I think we both know now who sent those texts."

"Yes, I think we do," Carolina confirmed.

When the police and FBI concluded their individual interview with Carolina she went up to her apartment, quickly stuffed her overnight case and garment bag with as much clothes and personal articles as she could. She knew she could never spend another night there again.

Before she left, she was assured by Inspector Miller that they would contact Karl's employees immediately. Carolina advised Miller that his employees were like family to him. She stated that 'the boys at Kaleidospokes were Karl's only family.'

CHAPTER 39

Carolina called Whitten and told him what happened and that she was heading to the *Post* to write her final article to this long saga. She affirmed that it would be in his inbox by four a.m. for editing, ready for the morning edition.

Indeed, her front page headline article entitled, *'THE END OF THE EVIL'* was in his inbox by four and subsequently in the hands of not just the reading citizens of Denver, but picked up by all of the national newspapers, and even all of the national TV and cable news outlets. She was a guest on every morning news show on every channel, including the one to which she would ultimately accept their offer for employment.

During the next few weeks, the FBI concluded their investigation and closed the case. Mayor Higgins was formally indicted, found guilty of multiple charges and sentenced to a minimum security prison in Idaho. Elizabeth Sanders was also found guilty of withholding evidence and an accessory to a crime, but because of the overlying circumstances the judge sentenced her to six months of house arrest and four years of probation.

As per Karl's wishes as described in his will and testament, he left the bicycle shop, Kaleidospokes to his four employees, all with equal shares.

Rebecca's touring bike was donated to the United States Bicyclist Hall of Fame museum, along with her plaque and a poignant biography of Rebecca Wilson as written by Carolina.

Carolina turned in her resignation to the *Post*, and stayed at a hotel until her commitments with them were satisfied. She returned to her folks in Indiana for a brief sabbatical, before heading to New York City to start her new career as an analyst at a leading cable news network.

Prior to her full-time analytical status, they networked her in slowly by having her do guest appearances and then substitute hosting on various shows on the network. This gave the viewing audience time to get familiar with her before giving her a timeslot.

On her first guest appearance at this network, she was asked by the host.' "*Was there any time through this whole escapade that you feared for your safety*"

Carolina thought for a moment then smiled when she recalled a quote from a relative who had long passed. She responded with,

"I WAS NEVER AFRAID!"

THE END

My inspiration for this fictional story, which you have just read is my late cousin Rebecca Jane Wilson. Despite never actually doing any of the afterlife antics, with which I took creative liberties, she did leave an indelible footprint on this planet, not just with her family, her friends and the people she would come to know, but also by the amazing trailblazing feats that she accomplished!

I have fond memories of my brother and I waiting for Cousin Becky, (my Grandfather's brother's daughter) to arrive during her famous 1967 trip across the United States. Two young boys spending a good portion of the day for nearly a month in lawn chairs positioned high on our rural Indiana hillside, so that we could be the first to spot her riding her bicycle down the state road to our house.

But not all my memories associated with Becky are fond. I also have a poignant memory burned into my brain of my Grandmother receiving a woeful call notifying her of Becky's tragic passing less than a year later after her visit.

On Bike, Killed

● Rebecca Wilson, 31, who crossed the U.S. twice on a bicycle, was injured fatally when a car struck her bike just 10 blocks from her Denver home. Miss Wilson quit her job at a Denver laundry in 1967 and set out for the West Coast on her racing bike. After reaching the coast, she doubled back across the country to New York City and then returned to Denver. The trip involved 7,300 miles of pedaling in 109 days.

REBECCA, *BECKY* JANE WILSON

Rebecca Wilson was born in Marion, Indiana May 26, 1937 to Wayne and Edith Wilson. The youngest of five children, she lost her mother at the tender age of eight years. Her father, distraught over his wife's death became unable to care for himself and his family and was temporarily placed in a sanitarium. Becky's older siblings were shuffled off to temporary foster homes, until family members could be notified. Becky was not so fortunate. As they couldn't find anyone to take her in, she accompanied her father. She had to endure the terrors of the asylum, until her father was deemed competent, and released under his own care.

Soon after his release, Wayne Wilson left Marion and traveled to Denver with Rebecca in tow.

There was a dreadful void left in Becky's life but she adapted as best she could. She finished grade school, then on to high school, where she graduated from Pueblo High School in 1956.

Soon after her high school graduation, Rebecca experienced another setback in her life by having a mental breakdown shortly after the passing of her father. *While gathering information for her bio, I came upon this very sad note from her personal journal.*

"I was to learn by bitter experience, the loneliness of those who are placed in a mental institution." ~ Becky Wilson

This set-back did not deter her steady rise over adversity. Fortunately her aunt Elizabeth Kenny who had been away for nearly a decade on a mission trip teaching in Kenya returned to the States and she took Becky under her wing. Elizabeth accepted a teaching position at the University of Nebraska and in 1962, Becky in turn enrolled at Union Community College in Lincoln.

During her stay with her aunt, she found Jesus, and as everyone does after accepting the Lord, her life immediately changed! Because she found peace, she found purpose and it was during that time she bought a bike from friends and began cycling.

Within a few weeks she was riding twenty to thirty miles a day. Then she discovered geared bikes and that was the beginning of what she believed to be her purpose in life.

She moved back to Denver, worked both at a laundry and a bicycle shop, saved her money and bought a racing bike. She began riding two hundred twenty miles a week, and riding fast, once being clocked over thirty-five MPH.

Rebecca became the first female member of the Denver Cycling Club and immediately outperformed her male counterparts. The Denver metro area soon became too small for her and she began trekking cross country. Admittedly she told a newspaper that being a lone female cyclist was not a very safe thing to do and wouldn't recommend it to youth. She advocated group riding for males or females wishing to follow in her footsteps, or in her case foot-pedals.

In 1966 she began training to be the first female to ride solo, consecutively across the United States and in 1967 she accomplished just that!

"I Was Never Afraid." This was an actual quote from Becky responding to a reporter's question, if she experienced any trepidation at anytime during her solo journey.

Becky traveled 7,300 miles in total, a trip that started from Denver, Colorado, to Los Angeles, California on the West Coast, back across the States to New York City on the East Coast, then doubling back across the country again to California, and finally concluding back in Denver. The journey took one hundred nine days.

She rode up and down mountains, across deserts and through rainstorms, sometimes on interstate highways and sometimes on narrow county roads, but her courage never wavered. She stayed overnight in homes, camped in her tent in parks and alongside roads.

In Iowa, on Interstate 80 she was pulled over by a highway patrolman for going under the 45 mph limit, he told her to exit the highway or he would arrest her. She waited for a bit until she thought he was out of the area then resumed her highway route. To her surprise as well as misjudgment he returned, arrested and fined her $10.00.

When she returned to Denver on her final leg of her historical ride, she was greeted by hundreds of fans. The Mayor proclaimed it *'Welcome Home to our Becky' Day!* Schools were closed, people lined the streets, both TV and print reporters were present for the homecoming fit for a dignitary.

With most, after accomplishing such a monumental feat they would have retired, but not Becky. She took a couple of weeks off then started training again. She had her sights on something bigger. Actually two things, Trying out for the 1970 U.S. Olympic Cycling Team, which she was, told she was a shoe-in and She wanted to fly to Fairbanks, Alaska and cycle all the way down to the Southern tip of South America. An accomplishment at the time no one else has ever done.

But on September 18, 1968 all of her quests ceased, as she was struck and killed by an automobile only ten blocks from her apartment.

Made in the USA
San Bernardino, CA
14 February 2018